COPY, KILL, REPEAT

STEVE CORNWELL

Copyright © 2025 Steve Cornwell

The right of Steve Cornwell to be identified as the Author of the Work has been asserted by them in accordance with the Copyright, Designs and Patents Act 1988.

First published in 2025 by Bloodhound Books.

Apart from any use permitted under UK copyright law, this publication may only be reproduced, stored, or transmitted, in any form, or by any means, with prior permission in writing of the publisher or, in the case of reprographic production, in accordance with the terms of licences issued by the Copyright Licensing Agency.

All characters in this publication are fictitious and any resemblance to real persons, living or dead, is purely coincidental.

www.bloodhoundbooks.com

Print ISBN: 978-1-917449-9-91

For my daughter,

*"Chase your dreams.
It's the only way to catch them."*

PROLOGUE

Sudo: Shipman, definitely Shipman…
    Jags: No way, man, you're dealing in numbers again, Sudo! It's about style, someone with a bit of finesse. Dahmer, that's your boy.
    Clown: What about Nilsen? Or Alfredo Ballí Treviño? The original Hannibal Lecter! A true legend. Sudo, why do you bother, you've no fucking idea!!
    Sudo: Fck you, clown! And Ed Gein was the original Lecter.
    Clown: You're mixing your films, Sudo. Gein was the basis for Psycho. Hannibal was inspired by Dr Treviño. And check your spelling, Sudo, there's no greater motive than bad punctuation, you know.

He had been going on for a little over three months now, and already they were in awe of him. His apparent unlimited knowledge and devotion to educate them had won them over immediately. Truth be told he'd found them by accident. Just a general surf, and there they were. A mongrel horde of internet lowlife, just waiting to be sculpted and manicured by his gentle persuasion. He had come in on a discussion of how one of them was planning the slaughter of his entire family. All rant no action. A teenager, no doubt about that. Such anger, such exuberance. Probably had his curfew reduced, or worse, grounded! For him it was a way to vent his anger, maybe for all of them. Would they ever realise that they now had a connoisseur among them? Someone with the experience they so craved. Someone who knew how it felt to look into the eyes of an individual as they drew their last breath. His fingers hovered over the keyboard, a pursed smile forming on his lips. He loved this. Watching them. Such pointless discussion. That would change, in time, but for now...

Tutor: Children, children. It's Jack. It will always be Jack.

It was time to teach.

CHAPTER ONE

"The victims of serial killers are all too often the throwaways of society. Who's going to notice them? Who is going to miss them?"

All eyes within the university auditorium were focused on him. They always were when he spoke. The girls gazed longingly, wanting to be with him, while the boys wanted to be him so they could have the girls look at them in the same way. At thirty-seven years old, he passed as mature without being old. An approachable mentor, rather than a stuffy lecturer. Never had a student willingly missed one of his lectures. Dr Ethan Marshall was known not only as an expert within his field, but also the most entertaining professor on campus. Mild mannered in his presentation and casually dressed in jeans and an open-collared shirt, it was where he felt most at ease. Exuding confidence, Ethan paced the stage gesticulating to give emphasis to his own opinions and beliefs in the benefits a criminologist can bring to both historical and current cases. His enthusiasm was infectious, and he loved looking out into the sea of faces, trying to pick out early, the students who could be the next Cesare Beccaria or J Edgar Hoover. The idea that someone within this theatre could be the reason a child lives, or a killer brought to justice, filled him with pride and a sense of purpose.

Despite the old Clifton building being full, even with students sat on the stairwells and lining the entrance landing, his voice echoed and reverberated around the historical walls. It was part of what made the college the place it was. The white walls, climbing high to lofty ceilings, lit by the rays of brilliant sunlight beaming through the shallow windows from the world outside. The intricate carvings that adorned the half pillars protruding from the wall along with the photos of the famous and scholarly that had previously been fortunate enough to reap the benefits of attending such an institution. A half moon of leather-bound seating, ascending skyward as if reaching for the heavens, towered awkwardly over the decked stage. For over eight hundred years the country's brightest minds had passed through the hallways and sat in the classrooms of this grand old campus. An image that never left Ethan's subconscious as he pictured the great students and lecturers that had resided on both sides of the invisible divide of student and teacher, feeling humbled to have stood alongside them and call them colleagues.

"If you are happy to play by numbers, then we could probably personify any current killer or rapist, currently avoiding capture, in the time we have left here today."

A sceptical few raised eyebrows amongst the gathered masses, but not one brave enough to interrupt or question the thinking of their lecturer. It had been done before, he would leave a thought hanging. Like a hook baited for the fish, waiting for a nibble of curiosity. A wry smile on Ethan's face put the audience at ease.

"But to do so would be dismissive, of both individuality and motive. Are the majority of serial killers sociopaths? Yes, they are. Have a large proportion come from broken homes, and been subject to abuse in one form or another as a child? Without a doubt. However, these are only the basis of what makes up a person capable of, what I hope everyone in here, could not even begin to think of acting out. Yet that is exactly what we are asking you to do. It is a fine line; we are asking you to think like them, without being like them. It is the reason why a number of previously enthused criminologists will burn themselves out and resort to training the great minds of tomorrow in some dated auditorium just to keep the wolves from the door and food on the table."

A ripple of laughter resonated around the hall as Ethan lifted himself onto the desk placed centrally on the stage, pushing down on his hands and swinging his legs back and forth, patiently waiting for the clamour to settle.

"We have seen, all too recently, how motive is becoming even more of a factor than previously contemplated. All too easily, a person's actions can be blamed on their mental health. And while this may still be true, in part, we need to accept that in certain instances the cause, and I use the word loosely, is the major factor for the news we all have to endure being reported from around the world."

A tentative hand raised in the third row. A young twenty-something student, demurely dressed. All eyes switched from the stage to the individual. Ethan waved invitingly, eager to hear some contribution.

"Terrorist attacks," she said shyly.

A nod of approval from Ethan.

"Go on," he asked.

Growing in confidence a little, the student straightened herself up in her seat.

"Well, they believe so emphatically in what they are doing that it cannot necessarily be put down to mental illness," she said more assertively.

"Not necessarily?" Ethan asked.

"No, because while an individual may believe without personal conflict, a number of those that execute those beliefs do so through fear or manipulation. It could be that they put the safety or security of their family and loved ones ahead of their own well-being or personal convictions. They could then be questioned on their mental state."

Ethan folded his arms and bit into his lower lip, allowing the rest of the students to take in what was being suggested.

"So where is the threat? Who do we focus our profiling on?" Ethan asked, raising his voice to now include the rest of the class once more.

Giving another nod of approval to the girl, Ethan pushed himself off the desk and began to pace the stage again, looking at the sea of faces in the room for some additional input.

"Both," said a deep voice toward the back of the auditorium. A breathless element to the suggestion, as a heavyset man walked along the entrance landing, stepping over students, to the top of the first set of stairs.

"The main concern is he, or she for that matter, with the heightened motive, but it would be foolish to not at least get an understanding of the weaker individuals. To gain an understanding of where and how the instigators are able to recruit their numbers. Then, in time, we have two options. We can, ideally, catch the perpetrator or we can cut off the supply chain which allows them to carry out their actions from a distance," continued the man, far too old to be a student himself.

Ethan stopped, a broad smile across his face, as the majority of students turned in their seats to study the man now standing at the top of the stairwell.

With an arm outstretched to introduce him, Ethan shook his head.

"Ladies and gentlemen, may I introduce you to Superintendent Meadows. If you hold up your end of the bargain over the next three years, you may just get to work closely with such a highly decorated individual."

"And if you hold up your end, Mr Marshall," Meadows mocked.

A few loose chuckles around the seating were met with Ethan's own laughter.

"That is very true," Ethan said, turning his attention back to his students.

"Anyway, I believe we shall call it to a halt there. Continue with the reading of the text previously set," he added, grabbing a book from the table and holding it aloft, "and I will look forward to seeing you all on Thursday."

A general rumble of noise grew as bags were collected and hundreds of feet all headed up the stairs toward the exits. Conversations growing in groups about what had just been discussed, while others made plans for the evening and days to come. Watching in a carefree state, Ethan rubbed his hands over his face and stretched his neck, taking in the view of the ceilings high above.

Fighting against the exodus of great young minds, Superintendent Meadows made his way down to the stage area, apologising as he knocked bags and students alike, gaining an ever wider berth as he progressed, until finally reaching his target.

"Ethan, still have them eating from that sweaty palm of yours then," he said, reaching out and shaking his friend's hand.

"Something like that. So, to what do I owe the pleasure of your company, Tony?"

Tony Meadows' expression dropped as he pondered over his opening gambit.

"We've got something we'd like you to take a look at, Ethan. Maybe a one-off, maybe not."

"I'm not sure it's me..." Ethan started as he gathered his bag from under the desk and began to pack items away.

"Please, Ethan, just a look," Tony replied, looking around the great empty room, now looking even bigger in its vacant state. "Somewhere a little less grand maybe," he continued.

Ethan paused, smiled at his friend and nodded, defeated.

Meadows looked around the perfectly kept office as he took a seat in the chair opposite Professor Marshall's nameplate and desk. The bookcases that lined the three walls were all full, but not a single binding looked out of place. All were stacked in order of size, looking as though they had never been touched. Superintendent Meadows knew different though. Ethan Marshall was, without question, the best profiler and criminologist he had ever worked with. He was, in fact, the very man who had won over an entire force, taking the role from publicity stunt to an essential part of a number of investigations that were coming up short. It was his profile that identified the outwardly affable childcare worker who had run a day nursery, as the prime suspect, and later convicted offender, on multiple child abuse charges. It pained him, however, that he needed him again. Whenever Ethan's particular expertise was required, it was always in regard to crimes of the very worst kind.

Ethan entered his office and handed a cup of tea to the superintendent.

"I can't vouch for the quality, but I know you're not here simply to catch up," he said, taking the seat behind his desk.

"Afraid not," Meadows responded solemnly. "We have a scene which, even though it was only called in this morning, we'd like you to... I'd like you, to take a look at and have an input in. You got plans for this afternoon?" he asked.

"Nothing of any great importance. You've got my attention though. So give me the overview," Ethan said.

Meadows puffed his cheeks out and slowly shook his head.

"I think it's best you see for yourself," he said, standing to his feet and considering whether a vending machine cup of tea was really strong enough for what lay ahead.

"I thought you meant photographs!"

"Please, Ethan, just a look," Meadows said, shrugging.

"Somewhere a little less grand maybe," Ethan said, raising his eyebrows.

"Indeed," Meadows confirmed gravely.

CHAPTER TWO

It had been as perfect as he could have imagined. No doubt they would have responded to the call by now. What a sight awaited them. He wished he could be there to see their faces. They would never admit it, and no doubt many would have claimed to have seen worse. But, admit it or not, they would be impressed by his work.

Every detail had been performed in almost ritualistic fashion. Attention to detail was one of his strengths and would be the reason that things were dictated at his pace. He was in no doubt that he was of superior intelligence. That was never to be questioned. Just look at their entry policy. Made easier year on year to fight the ever increasing tide of depleting recruitment numbers. Firstly, a little less fit. Like the career criminals are letting themselves slip and that isn't so important. How many kept themselves in that shape anyway? Lowering the bar just means that there isn't as far to fall. Then, in line with the rest of the nation, intellect is overrated, so ask fewer questions, and make them multiple choice too. A motley crew of school dropouts and wannabe military types not cut out for the art of war. Criminals never had it so good. Maybe they wouldn't see things that way. That was understandable. For now.

The apartment was small but not cramped. A modern two-bedroom in the heart of the city was never going to offer floorspace as a selling point. Clinically kept though, every room had an air of show-home about it. He moved from room to room with ease, stopping only to flick off a light, accidentally left on in the hallway. Selecting a clean shirt from the wardrobe, he moved through to the kitchen where the ironing board was already set up and the radio played. Listening intently to the debate on how child killers should be tried after another incident had recently left the nation in shock, he filled the water jug, making sure not to spill a drop on the shiny granite surfaces.

"*If they are capable of doing what they did, why are they not capable of taking responsibility? Hanging is too good for the likes of these. Yet no doubt they will get their bed, board and new console to play on before being out within a couple of years. Where is the justice for the victim's family?*"

"*But many of these people, and they are people, however you wish to label them, are victims themselves. Products of their own upbringing,*" the guest expert stated.

"*So you're saying that their behaviour is acceptable?*" the radio presenter asked in an overtly bewildered manner.

"*Of course it isn't acceptable. Conversely it is understandable–*"

"*That's bullshit,*" the caller interrupted.

"*Caller, please, apologies to our listeners.*"

"*Sorry, but to say acting out in such a way is understandable is complete bull. There are plenty of people whose daddy handed them a beating when they were younger, is it acceptable that all of these act out without rationale? And you, you who defend them and keep them on the streets are just as bad, taking a payday and putting the public at risk on an ongoing basis. It's a fucking joke. Heaven forbid you should ever end up a casualty of one of society's victims,"* he ranted.

"Well, apologies again," the presenter said, cutting off the caller. *"A controversial subject which does emit emotion from all. We'll rejoin with the honourable Owen Hammond and you, after this."*

As the voices from the radio faded out, The Who's 'The Kids Are Alright' began to fill the kitchen.

Smiling at what he hoped was purposeful irony, he pressed the iron down heavily onto the pristine white shirt. Creases perfectly aligned. It could be a new shirt straight from the wrapping. That was what the people at work always said. Flawlessly presented, polite, but not overly social. A line lifted directly from his most recent appraisal. They said it like a criticism. It was his place of work, nothing more. He had friends, plenty of them. And they would argue that he was very social.

Slipping on his shirt, he buttoned it methodically, moved out to the front door, slipped on his jacket and headed out into the city for what would surely be another eventful evening.

CHAPTER THREE

Competing with North London traffic at any time was a chore, on a Friday at around four o'clock it was something to be strictly avoided. There had been very little chat throughout the entire journey. Superintendent Meadows' demeanour had changed as soon as they started heading south. While the engine of his Jaguar XJ purred along, all Ethan could do was take in the passing sights and sounds and wonder exactly what was awaiting him. They had worked their way down the A10, passing through the greenest of country, seeing field after field being harvested, into the more urban, harsher environment of outer London. It had been one of the major factors in moving from the city. A nicer, softer environment in which to grow as a family. Attitudes changed as you approached the City. People walked with a more visible outlook, a greater sense of purpose. Groups of youths sauntered the streets of Enfield as the car crawled from one set of traffic lights to the next, struggling with the exasperating three lanes to two at every junction, punishing any vehicle over the size of a Mini Cooper who foolishly expected a London driver to allow them to feed in a car at a time. Whoever had come up with this ingenious road layout clearly hadn't foreseen how the mindset of even the most English of gentlemen would evolve to cope with modern-day rush hour traffic. Straight from school, home, and out to meet up with friends. Ethan wondered why so many chose to spend their evenings on street corners, or in front of parades of shops. Was the desire to stay away from home so great? Time and again, the importance of a stable family background would be discussed during his lectures, or be highlighted as a missing factor when assisting in a current investigation. Were we now moving toward the type of society where we engineered solidarity? The lone wolf syndrome, in group effect?

"Nearly there," Meadows husked, breaking the silence.

The recently retired racing stadium of Walthamstow coming into view in the near distance. Another redundant representation of what was once a vibrant hub on the outskirts of London left to ruin along with much of the surrounding neighbourhoods.

"You still enjoy the odd punt?" Meadows asked, trying to lighten his own mood.

Ethan's smile grew as he looked over at the dilapidated stadium, imagining it on a Friday night when he and his wife would march alongside the throb of an ever-hopeful crowd. The stags and the hens out on the start of what would be a long evening. The masses on a night out, and the desperate, whose conviction that the evening's results would improve their own lives beyond comprehension never failed to be infectious.

"Now and again," Ethan replied.

"Right!" Meadows said, chuckling.

As the Jaguar eased through the side streets at a low hum, Ethan took in the changing landscape. Seeing first the number of for sale signs increase, and then into a mix of the uninhabitable and the homes of those who had simply given up on the idea that anyone would choose to move here.

"A rough-looking suburb of London. How clichéd!" Ethan quipped.

Meadows grunted in agreement, turning right onto a tight-looking road with cars parked either side. Pulling up outside one of the only terraces on the street not boarded up, Ethan was met with the familiar blue-and-white tape barrier, crackling as it caught every breeze passing over it. Two officers stood outside the front door who offered a cursory nod upon seeing the superintendent. The SOCO team were already in full swing, moving in and out of the house at increased regularity, working in unison like an army of white ants. Bagged evidence and samples transferred from scene to vehicle with care and precision, each item with the potential to show a little more image of the overall puzzle.

"Who says London has to be expensive?" Ethan said.

"Well, I can't see this pushing the prices up. Help yourself." Meadows gestured for Ethan to enter the house. "Straight through. I don't want to influence you on this one," he continued.

Ethan moved hesitantly through the front door into the dingy hallway. Ripped carpet showed the way, worn stairs to the left made their way up into the dark, a diminutive kitchen without units and smelling of mould on the right. Straight ahead was the lounge, a murmur of activity as the crime-scene team moved across his line of vision. He had observed dozens of scenes like this, some too gruesome to make it into horror films. Yet this was the first time since that virgin visit that he had felt any kind of nerves. His stomach had bottomed out and he could hear his own breathing deepen, trying to regulate the adrenaline being released. A collective silence filled the floor as he took his first steps into the room. A stranger who looked like he belonged. As Meadows came into view and gave his silent approval, the bustle of activity returned. Ethan was instantly reaching for breath, his lungs suddenly deflated by an invisible punch, a heavy weight bearing down deep upon his chest. It wasn't the act or the heinous nature of what he was looking at, he had seen far worse in his time. It was more to do with the scene itself, the familiarity of it all. He had witnessed this very scene before, and on so many occasions. Just never quite so real, so lifelike. Ethan jumped as a hefty hand sat on his right shoulder.

"A blast from the past, right?" Meadows whispered.

"Do you think someone is trying to get our attention?" he asked.

Ethan shook his head in wonder trying to take it all in, eyes wide, swallowing hard to try and salivate his dry mouth.

"Obviously the body has had to be moved. We'll catch up with him down at the morgue later on. But if you put that back in the picture, middle of the floor, facing upwards, what have you got?" Meadows continued.

"A little piece of history," Ethan said softly, rubbing a hand over his mouth.

Mentally removing every member of the crime team, and placing the body as Meadows had described, Ethan tried to create an accurate mental image of how this would have been found earlier that day...

More worn carpet, bare to the floor in places. Wallpaper peeling away both top and bottom, with large patches of damp climbing the walls and discolouring the once white ceiling. The furniture dated and in no better condition than the rest of the room. Torn upholstery, cigarette burns and stained cushions. Whoever it was that lived here was not the house-proud type. An old television sat atop a pile of magazines and had a crack across the front screen, wires trailing loose to sockets that had been ripped from the wall. That would've been enough to put off any prospective purchaser. The activities of the day would ensure another building was boarded up in the very near future. The walls looked as if it had rained red as blood spatter covered the decrepit décor in slashes. No wall had been spared. A lot of anger had spent time in this room. A body lay in the middle of the room, blankly staring at the ceiling, arms and legs splayed at painful angles. Multiple puncture wounds throughout the body, lacerations on the arms from futile attempts at defence. Deep bruising also, on both the upper torso and cranial area, now bled out onto the carpet. And, away from the victim, pasted on the left wall, facing out of the netted bay window, in what would appear to be blood, was the word '*PIG*' in lettering about a foot high.

Coming back to the present, Ethan took a deep breath and exhaled slowly, puffing out his cheeks.

"Definitely wants our attention," Ethan said.

Meadows moved steadily around the room making sure to avoid the SOCO team as they continued with their evidence-gathering, cutting away a sample of the worn carpet for further analysis.

"Obviously we'll know a little more once we get all this back to the labs and get some answers regarding DNA and timeline estimates from the autopsy. Not a pretty picture though, is it?" he asked.

"Accurate though. It's as if it's been lifted from one of the college textbooks. If you ignore that this is a London dumping ground, and not an LA mansion of course," Ethan said, starting to trace Meadows' footsteps to take a closer look at the area where the body had lain.

Meadows turned to face Ethan, raising his eyebrows.

"Initial thoughts? Before we head over to the morgue," he asked.

"Well, if simply stating the obvious, it's a copycat murder. It's a tribute to the Manson family murders. From the frenzied spatter of the blood on the walls, to the smeared message. It's a male, of high intelligence, over thirty, and I would say under fifty. He's methodical. This takes planning, and despite the scene suggesting otherwise, he would have had to exude calmness in order to have the attention to detail that we recognise what he was trying to express. And he'll kill again. You don't go to the trouble of what we see here for a one-off. Sadly, this will be the start of something. And unless stopped, it may not have a fixed end date. This is someone who will be enjoying what they are doing. I would also reason that this isn't personal, he won't have known the victim, other than for the purpose he served today."

Meadows nodded as he moved back through the room toward the hallway, motioning for Ethan to follow him.

"Well, that's the teaser, now let's go check out the support cast in this little play. DI Swift will meet us there. She's going to be heading this one up," Meadows said as they made their way out of the property, ready to rejoin the stationary movement of the London rush hour.

Ethan followed, calling after his friend, "Tony, I…"

Meadows turned, smiling. "Just a look, Ethan."

Ethan returned the smile and shaking his head made his way to the passenger side of the car.

CHAPTER FOUR

DI Swift hated this place. It was one thing to see what one person was capable of doing to another, but to go and watch someone dismantle a body turned her stomach. However, after being on scene earlier on, she was intrigued to discover what the pathologist could gleam off a corpse in such a state.

I'd like to see what they come up with as the cause of death on this one, she thought as she made her way across the car park to the gloomy concrete edifice. Why the outside of these buildings had to be as morbid as the inside baffled her. A lick of paint could do wonders for this building. And why Lucy wanted to work in such an environment puzzled her even more. It was the last place you would imagine her, with her bubbly personality and 'glass half full' philosophy. Whoever said opposites attract couldn't have asked for a stronger argument to their case. Pushing through the heavy double swing doors into the hospital-like passageways, DI Swift took the all too well-known route to room 3a to hear once more what the worst of society could lower themselves to.

Ethan, Tony Meadows and Lucy Quest, the pathologist,

were already finishing off introductions as DI Swift made her way into the room.

"Hey, Luce," Swift said.

DI Swift and Lucy had joined the force in their corresponding positions around the same time. In what remained a male-dominated profession it hadn't taken them long to find one another and seek solace in a like-minded soul. Although facing their own difficulties and professional hardships as they fought for acceptance, it was nice to have a female view on things, rather than trying to always be a member of the Boys' Club. What had been a friendship of convenience initially, Lucy would now be the one person Swift would turn to, should she ever need anything.

"Sir," she said, acknowledging Meadows also.

"Hey, Abbey, how's it treating you?" Lucy asked.

"No complaints, still enough bad guys to keep us in the game," she replied.

Meadows coughed and motioned toward Abbey Swift.

"Ethan Marshall, meet DI Abbey Swift; Abbey, Ethan," he introduced.

The pair shook hands. Ethan taken a little aback by just how attractive the DI was. Did she simply look good or were officers getting promoted younger these days?

"So you're the mind guy, eh? Through the eyes of a killer and all that," Abbey ribbed with a grin, before turning her attention back to the central slab.

"Something like that," Ethan retorted, liking the new DI immediately.

"Maybe not," Lucy interrupted.

Lucy turned to her audience of three who were looking at her in slight confusion, waiting for her to elaborate. Enjoying the moment, Lucy walked round the slab, before turning round to walk in the opposite direction when her way was blocked by the three visitors, tapping her fingers together as if in thought as she walked, a playful smile on her face.

"Let me walk you through it," she said. "As you can see, the victim, who, for the record, is a white male, approximately sixty-five to seventy years of age, has been beaten, has multiple stab wounds, bludgeoning lesions to the head and for good measure was shot four times in the face from close range," she continued.

"A replica of the Manson family killings. Followed to the letter in fact," Ethan cut in.

"Your area of expertise, Professor, so I shall take your word for it. However, I have a couple of questions for you. Firstly, what is missing from this picture?" she asked, turning to focus her attention on the elderly male while looking up his body from the feet end of the slab.

"And secondly, what was attributed to the cause of death at the original crime that captured our killer's imagination so?" Lucy asked, still enjoying the moment, letting a silence linger as the three of them took a more detailed view of the body in front of them, Ethan wondering why the exact cause of death held any relevance. Abbey's eyes suddenly lit up as she moved along the body looking at the arms lying motionless on the cold stone.

"He hasn't got any defensive wounds. Not a single one!" she said in astonishment.

Ethan and Meadows moved along the body meticulously, leaning in closer to inspect the unscathed arms, waiting for a wound to reveal itself.

"He suffered all of this abuse, and never once did he try and protect himself," she continued.

Nodding in approval, Lucy turned to Ethan, simply tilting her head and raising her eyebrows. A look of bewilderment, Ethan shook his head.

"I'm struggling for the significance, but I guess, despite the beating, pistol-whipping and numerous stab wounds, the fatal blow is accepted to probably have been the first gunshot to the face," he explained.

"Though in truth it could have been any of the four or a culmination of all of them," he said.

"But not a heart attack?" Lucy quizzed.

Meadows had been listening intently, as was his way. He would always be the last to react in any given situation, but he would always be the best informed, and when he did react, he did so with absolute confidence and conviction in his own actions. Stepping in front of both Ethan and Abbey he placed his hands on the slab, next to the body, leaning over the old man but all of his focus solely on Lucy Quest.

"You're telling me he died of a heart attack?" he hissed.

"And that time of death was at least three days prior to the visible injuries you see before you," Lucy explained calmly.

A stunned silence filled the morgue. Ethan shook his head with minimal motion, perplexed, as he started to walk alongside the length of the body, the echoes of each step resonating off the walls.

"Everything you see before you was done post mortem. The blood has already clotted, so I'm guessing the wall dressing you described at the scene won't belong to our victim here," Lucy continued as she turned to Ethan. "And while he may have recreated an atrocious crime scene with great accuracy, he has one major disparity from the original perpetrator."

Lucy paused for effect, still enjoying the confusion her findings had caused.

"We can't say that he has actually ever killed anyone. You may not even be looking for a murderer," she informed them.

"Which just makes the overall message all the more significant," Ethan said. "This is a lot of work," he continued, "which would suggest what is to follow will only increase in magnitude."

"You sound impressed," Abbey said, distinctly un so.

"How can you not be," Ethan concluded.

A dense silence fell in the room once more, leaving only a cold chill and a hundred unanswered questions lingering in the air and the minds of those present.

CHAPTER FIVE

Tutor: It's because it is human nature to be careless. Everyone knows the usual candidates, but that is mainly down to their failings. Because they allowed themselves to be caught. It is therefore pragmatic to assume that the greatest icons of all time will never be known. Remaining faceless, their work speaking for them, that is what should be strived for.

Slash: Everyone gets caught, Tutor. That's the only reason the desires on here are kept in check.

Tutor: Risk and reward, Slash. That is where the excitement lies. Therein lies the challenge. And not everyone gets caught. In fact, nobody need get caught. The Zodiac Killer, Jack the Ripper, the Alphabet Killer or the real JFK shooter. Only difference was they took the time and effort to make themselves anonymous.

Jags: Is this from experience, Tutor? How would you ensure you evaded capture?

He stood from the desk and decided now would be the time to let them fill his self-imposed abstaining from the forum. No doubt they would speculate on whether he was capable, whether he had done what, in cyberspace at least, they all claimed to have the will to perform. It had been years since he had first looked into the eyes of a soul as it made the transition of incumbent to spirit. The excitement of that initial experience still thrilled him, but the need to heighten the sensation had been burrowing away within him for too long. Eating into his very essence like a disease that needed to be cut out, a hunger that could never be satisfied or a thirst that could not be quenched. All the preparation of the last few months would soon come to fruition, and the pleasure echelon would be overwhelming.

He walked barefoot, silently around the apartment in the dark. The only light being the radiant glow of the screen from the box bedroom, acting as a study, reaching through to the hallway. The dull drone of countless processors whirring away beneath, hidden from view. Outside he could hear the distant sounds of police sirens travelling away to an unknown destination while the services of the capital spread out to multiple callings. Another busy night on the streets of the city. It may just be a domestic abuse case, the cowards of society with nothing but time and violence on their minds. Alternatively, it could be a situation resolved with biblical justice. Do unto others, an eye for an eye. The thought of what others may be acting out on this very night energised him, and the adrenaline and excitement spread throughout his body. He considered retiring to the bedroom and relieving himself of the tension. Suddenly he hit himself, hard, across the chest, and again, and again. It was that kind of weakness that broke an individual. It was the ability to separate yourself from emotion and act with precision that would result in the high far greater than any cheap moment of ecstasy. Taking a glass from the cupboard he poured himself water from the tap and dampened his brow, before composing himself and returning to the computer screen.

He settled back into the deep leather chair and read the reaction to his short hiatus.

Sudo: Tell us then, Tutor. Are you speaking from experience?

Slash: Of course not. Tutor, you are so full of shit! All talk. I don't know how you got some of these on here thinking you're something special. You're nothing, a nobody.

The greatest trick the devil ever produced was convincing the world he didn't exist, he thought. This new boy could be an issue. The others were followers. This one could think for himself, and ultimately that meant he could influence others. The thought irked him, an issue that would need to be nipped in the bud.

Sudo: Bad call, Slash, he's the real deal.

Slash: Real Deal!!!! He has done nothing but talk, what has he shown you? Any of us could describe an event. It's pure fantasy. Just because he's articulate (it means well-read and educated, Sudo!) you lot follow him like the Second Coming.

Jags: No one asks you to stick around, Slash. If we are such a bunch of sheep, why not get your kicks elsewhere?

Clown: I'm with Sudo. A definite aficionado. We should be grateful he stays on here. If it's ever to be more than desires, then he is the one entity that can teach.

Slash: Aficionado? Entity? You are even starting to sound like him. Bunch of no-brain robots. There is no such thing as the perfect murder.

Their defence of him was touching, though truth be told Slash's description of them as a whole wasn't too wide off the mark. But wasn't that the beauty of them. Conversation had moved somewhat off track though. With a heavy sigh, he picked up the glass of water, wiping away the water ring below the glass and cursing himself for lack of a coaster, lifted himself from his seated position and headed for the doorway, leaving the computer running. He could catch up on any late-night discussions in the morning. As he reached the doorway, shutting his mind's activities down in preparation for some much needed sleep, a high-pitched bleep from behind caught his attention and he turned his head back toward the screen. A little flashing icon had appeared on the bottom right of the display. An intrigued frown rippled across his forehead as he softly made his way back to the chair. A little red PM continued to flash from within its little black surrounding. He moved the cursor over the icon and clicked. The icon expanded to fill the screen.

Private Message
 From:Clown
 To:Tutor
 Ref:So how could we do it?
 ????

A dispassionate grin stretched across his face. How could *we* do it? Things had just moved on. Maybe even a little quicker than he had been hoping for.

CHAPTER SIX

Superintendent Meadows leant back on the table, a whiteboard behind him, showing only the beaten face of the newly named victim, if indeed he could be called a victim. He looked out over the incident room, at full capacity with officers, administrators, senior leaders and one criminologist. The case, even though still in its infancy, had captured the imagination of the station. Abuse, rape and murder were sadly commonplace. No one would flinch over another John Doe being found dumped along the side of the road, even if they were in a full-size chicken costume with a note saying why they'd tried to cross. Like all the major cities of the world, London was full of the eccentric. Someone could always explain their motive for anything. And that was fine. Close the case and on to the next. But a dead body, at a murder scene with no murder. That was different. Everyone wanted to know of any progression or newly discovered lead. Meadows feared this may be a far longer drawn-out investigation than he or anyone else present in the room was hoping for. With targets raised and manpower reduced the last thing he wanted was another major case within the capital. Statistics were everything, and this was clearly not going to improve his. Taking another look around the room and pulling his ample frame to its maximum height, he addressed the room.

"Arthur Green, seventy-two years old, lived alone in the Edmonton area, a widower of some twelve years. A regular at the local crown bowls club, and a voice of reason to the youth of his neighbourhood. Another victim who no one has a bad word to say about. More importantly though, he died of a heart attack at least three days before we found him," he stated.

Meadows paused for the inevitable murmur around the room, even though everyone present was well aware of this little revelation relating to the case. As the room settled once more, he cleared his throat and continued.

"Which, considering the beating and abuse his body took after that, has to be considered a blessing. The facts are as follows. Arthur Green's corpse was taken, exactly when we do not yet know, placed in a close to derelict property and beaten, stabbed and shot four times in the head from point-blank range. The scene left no indication of who the assailant was, no prints, no fibres. The blood that covered the room was from multiple contributors. And the small element that we were able to lift, having avoided cross-contamination, all came back as donor unknown. No records in the system for any of them. And the kicker as per, is that of course nobody local, saw or heard anything," he finished, sighing defeatedly at the all too familiar ending of his summation.

The room burst into a hubbub of conversations all breaking out at the same time. Over the noise a young officer stood and called out to bring the room into silence.

"So are we looking at multiple offenders then, with the number of bloods present?" he asked.

"It certainly isn't something we can rule out, but we believe not," Meadows rebutted as he waved for Ethan to join him at the front of the assembly.

Another breakout of noise as Ethan made his way forward, an unknown face to most, yet a well-known reputation throughout the station.

"I would ask you though to direct early character questions to Mr Ethan Marshall. He will be assisting us, if willing, as the investigation unfolds," Meadows said, more asking Ethan than addressing those in front of him.

"Can't we just leave this to real policework then, sir," an officer said from a small gathering towards the back of the room. "Or are we required to be exploring all avenues to appease the media? My old lady knows a psychic whack-job if we really need some help," he continued, drawing a minority of mirth from within the group.

"He's here because I want him here. Is that okay with you, officer?" Meadows husked through gritted teeth.

"Let us not forget it is you who is here through division, Bridkins, no one else."

Division was a polite way of saying IOPC without actually naming names and embarrassing an individual further. The Independent Office for Police Conduct wasn't a body any serving officer wanted attributed to their name. As with any workplace, gossip could become gospel, and mud stuck, leaving reputations tainted.

Bridkins fell back into the pack of bodies around him, doing his best to hide the embarrassment of being shot down as those close to him distanced themselves by placing all their attention to the man introduced at the front of the room.

Ethan smiled and then addressed the room giving the basic overview he had provided to the superintendent earlier on at the crime scene. Having a recent history within the station and successfully assisting on other high-profile cases, Ethan spoke in the same relaxed manner he would when teaching one of his classes. The attention from the majority in attendance was without question and simply confirmed the high regard he was generally held in by a force looking to comprehend how best to understand the thinking patterns of the criminal fraternity.

Bridkins and what would appear to now be just one or two followers found more interest in what was happening on the streets outside of the station.

As Ethan finished, Superintendent Meadows stepped to the fore once more, giving instructions to a section of the room to concentrate on who Arthur Green was, who were his friends, what routines did he follow and most importantly whether his body was obtained through planning or fortuitous coincidence.

"Check missing persons around the area. That much blood had to come from somewhere. We have nothing to rule out that it could be from other victims. We may be sure that this wasn't a murder, but that isn't to say there hasn't been at least one, if not more! Right people, let's get going," Meadows concluded as he dismissed everyone from the room, leaving just he and Ethan along with DI Swift. All silently hoping that someone leaving that room could uncover an intimation of what was to come, rather than having to react after the event.

"We could do with some help on this one, Ethan. If you're interested," Meadows asked, turning to his friend.

"That all right with you, Swift?" Meadows asked, more as what was going to happen than a question.

"Not a problem with me, sir. I just want to get this one sorted quickly," Abbey said with a smile. "And we can do that can't we, Doc?" she asked, openly rhetorical.

"I'll need to arrange cover at the college, but that won't be a problem. Plus you and he have got my interest now," Ethan answered, talking to the superintendent but looking at Abbey, causing her to redden ever so slightly.

"All right then, you sort your students out and get back here as soon as you can, although I can't guarantee the tea will be as good as you're used to," Meadows said with a mischievous grin.

The bronzed plaque on the dense wooden door read *Superintendent Tony Meadows* but the office behind was not that of an organised high-ranking officer. Abbey was always amazed how her superior could have such a sharp, well-ordered mind, and work out of such chaos. The walls were adorned with pictures, but not of awards or commendations as she had seen in other senior official offices. Tony Meadows was an American sports enthusiast, and his office portrayed his passion. Famous Superbowl pictures were hanging next to photos of the superintendent and Patrick Ewing and the rest of the great New York Knicks team of the nineties. A signed boxing glove, once belonging to Mike Tyson stood in a glass case in the corner of the room, his most prized of possessions, polished so the glass gleamed. All the memorabilia was in exquisite condition and would no doubt fetch an impressive bid should the superintendent ever fall on hard times and seek out the auction houses. The paperwork, however, was not so cared for. Mountains of paper and forms awaiting completion poured over the top of the numerous in-trays on the desk and atop of filing cabinets. The desk itself was hidden from view, under an abundance of lever arch files, just the remnants of a computer keyboard showing through the office debris, resting in front of the monitor.

"Sorry to keep you, Swift," Meadows said, marching into the room, throwing his jacket onto the sofa to the right of his office.

"No worries, sir. I was just admiring your filing. I've got a stack of it should you want to pass on your secret."

"No secret. I know where everything is in this room. Should

I need it, it's just an arm's length away. You see a mess, I would argue different. Got to keep the advantage, especially with you youngsters so keen to advance these days," he continued. "Sit, sit." He gestured.

Abbey moved another couple of folders from the chair onto the floor, tutting as she did so.

"I heard that," Meadows said. "So, you all right having Ethan working alongside you?" he asked.

"I said it was fine, why does everyone think I'd have a problem working with him?" she snapped, her mood changing to the defensive.

"Not him, particularly, you just give the impression that you're happiest when left to your own devices. And don't get me wrong, I've known plenty others like that, and if it gets results, you'll hear no complaints from me," he argued.

"Why do people think that? Why would I not want someone like Ethan, if he can help?" she asked.

"You weren't happy with Parkinson or Smyth and..."

"That's because they were Muppets, not because I didn't want a partner. I just don't want to be babysitting a twenty- or even thirty-something," she interrupted sharply. "And anyway, Ethan's..."

"Hmmm, he's," Meadows teased with an inquisitive beam.

"Different," Abbey said cautiously. "So what's his story anyway?"

Meadows ran a hand over his face, reminding himself that he was well overdue a shave, leant back in his chair and rested his hands on his head, taking a deep breath and exhaling.

"Well, we're lucky that he is still available to us, really. I guess his inquisitive nature and fascination in the worst civilisation has to offer was too much for him. He had carved out quite an impressive record of profiling serial killers and being accredited with honours for the incarceration of some of our more recent infamous celebrities. One of those cases being the Railway Killer, about six years ago," Meadows explained.

"I know the one, targeted young female students, would rape and torture them for a couple of days then leave their bodies on the tracks in the tunnels to destroy evidence," she said.

"The very one. Well, it was thanks in no small part to one Ethan Marshall that he was caught and convicted," Meadows continued. "The young Mr Marshall was lauded for his intellect and insight, meaning he got both televised minutes and column inches."

"A celebrity then?" Abbey asked.

"Of sorts. However, the one person who wasn't so impressed with our professor was the mother of the accused who initially preached his innocence to all those that would listen, and then, outside the courthouse, threatened to take away the thing Ethan cared about most, seeing as he had done just that to her. Not much attention was paid to such an idle threat. Just a woman grieving for her son's lost freedom, and her refusal to see past the image of her little boy."

Meadows stretched and puffed out his cheeks, an awkward smile on his lips, attempting to put himself and Abbey at ease, trying hard to swallow the lump forming in his throat before he continued.

"Three months later there was a break-in at Ethan's home while he was away, and his wife was shot by the mother before she turned the gun on herself. Their baby was on her own, at just eight months, for almost two days. She spent a while in hospital but came through it unscathed as much as they can tell. No way she could've seen anything," he concluded solemnly.

Abbey had a sharp intake of breath as her eyes widened.

"And now?" she asked.

"Now he looks after his little girl with the help of his wife's mother, who is a widow herself. They've needed each other to get through, but since working at the college and returning to the fold from a distance with some of the recent cases over the past couple of years, he is something like his old self."

An uncomfortable silence filled the office, both staring into an empty space, ensuring eye contact was avoided. Meadows was controlling his breathing, though it was still audibly heavier than normal as he tried to hold his emotions intact.

"So that's your new partner. And if you tell him you know any of what I just said, I can guarantee you will be looking at at least a couple of reductions in pay grade," he warned, a mix of mood-lightening and threat in his voice.

CHAPTER SEVEN

The private messages had continued over the last couple of nights, gentle persuasion on how evasion was a simple goal and the act itself was more calculated than emotional. Emotion was the reason people got caught. Allowing emotion to get involved led to mistakes. Although wary of the short time to have elapsed, he decided tonight would be the time to chance his arm and make the subtle proposal that they turn their discussions to reality. If the reaction wasn't what was expected he could always pass it off as affable bravado, most of those on here were all talk. But he felt good, confident that he had read him right. His only concern was time. He wanted to do this correctly, ensure everything was in place before he started his shift. Already dressed, he needed to be ready when the time called, but for now, he had more important things to concentrate on.

Tutor: So, have you thought about it? Completing your education.

Clown: I'm nervous. I want to, and I don't want to let you down.

Perfect. It wasn't a no. This one genuinely wanted to take the next step. Wanted to try and feed the hunger that burned inside him. A hunger that until now he no doubt feared was his alone. He knew he had to tread carefully now. The seed had been sown. Now he had to help it grow, nurture it. He could feel the broad smile across his face as he typed, and the beads of sweat forming on his brow as his hands started to feel clammy, a mixture of anticipation and excitement. Control the emotion, he thought to himself. Just control the emotion.

Tutor: The nerves are good. They will keep you concentrated. I'll walk you through. We'll do this together. And then you can feel how I did, still do. The feeling lasts for days.
 Clown: Still do? When did you last, DO IT?

The coverage had been minimal compared to his expectations. Maybe they had been holding back so not to cause panic in a city already gripped by the fear of where the next crazed killer or terrorist attack was coming from. Ever since terrorism had become mainstream, the nation had to be treated with kid gloves. World economics could be affected simply by the very threat of an impending attack. Never mind the attacks themselves, and the atrocities they had caused, the fear, the ever-prevailing fear, that was the terrorist cells' real mark of success. The effort he had put in deserved to be recognised on a grander scale, but that would come. It had been enough, however, to have made it onto the forums and get his minions talking. And now, having not joined in, he could show his hand by using Clown as his confidante. And also set the stage and tone of what he expected in return.

Tutor: I shouldn't. This would be a huge trust I place in you.

He left it two or three minutes before returning to the keyboard. He liked to imagine the level of expectation at the other end of their invisible connection. Could Clown contain his eagerness and wait out the silent period in the hope of gaining such trust?

Tutor: A few days gone now. You've even spoken of your admiration of the act. I was too embarrassed to reply. But your kind words flattered me.
Clown: The Manson copy?!? No Way! You are fucking unreal. That was genius.
Tutor: Like I said, I am trusting you with this. There is no one else I could do that with. I hope I haven't misplaced my faith in you.

Clown, or Danny Jemson, as he was known outside of his virtual reality, sat open-jawed looking at the screen in front of him. He knew this guy was the real thing, but to be online with him, it was beyond exciting. If he felt like this now, how would he feel joining him? And he had picked him, out of all of them, he had chosen him. Tutor had seen in him what he wanted to see in himself. An inner strength to act out his deepest desires. She was going to realise now what he was capable of. Why couldn't she have just given them a bit longer. Too old to be living at home she said. When was he going to grow up and make something of himself, for them, for himself? How long was he going to live off others and be happy being nothing?

They had met on a night out, and hit it off immediately. For six months it had been absolute bliss, like something out of a movie. Nights out with friends, pubs, clubs, concerts, and even more fun, the nights in at her apartment. Then overnight, fun wasn't enough, he wasn't enough. She was about to finish her degree and ready to go out into the world and make something of herself. Was he coming with her? Did he have it in him to keep up with her? That's when the rows started. Her and her friends saying he needed to prove he wanted to be in a proper relationship. Talking to him like he was a child. Telling him he had to make something of himself.

"We'll see who makes something of themselves," he said under his breath as he primed himself for a life-altering decision.

Clown: Ok, I'm in. When are we going to do it?

He breathed out slowly and softly, a relief more than anything. The effort to seek out the right individual had paid off. Surely it was just a matter of encouraging him through now.

Tutor: Soon, but be patient, we need to decide how, more importantly.
Clown: As painful as possible, this bitch deserves everything she gets.

He shook his head, he had to calm him down. Emotion, or lack of it was everything. He could not allow a petty personal issue derail his vision, not when he was so close.

Tutor: No! Anonymity is the aim. You let sentiment or feeling get involved and you can think about spending the rest of your life in a prison cell. Something that should appeal to no one. You are about to ascend above the law, not be answerable to it. I can provide you with everything you need. We'll arrange a point where you can collect your tools. Like I said, I'll walk you through it. All you have to do is choose the victim. Someone faceless. The missable of society. They are the key to our ongoing success.

Clown: A hooker. Just like the bitch.

The response came up instantaneously which impressed him.

Tutor: Perfect. There is one other thing I ask of you though.

He finished typing out the instructions and made Danny recall everything in detail. He knew he could just read it from previous conversation, but retyping would help it all sink in. Detail was important, and Danny had been eager to take it all in and impress with the speed of his response. He hadn't needed to go over the text from earlier. Satisfied he had covered everything, it was now in the hands of his newly found protégé. A knock on the door snapped him from his musings and startled him out of his seat as he tried to push thoughts of what was going to take place from his mind. He flicked off all the lights, closed each door, enjoyed the silence and made his way down the stairs to the front entrance, opening the door to the familiar face of his work colleague, Mike Naylor.

"Thanks for this, Mike, much appreciated," he said.

Mike had already turned and was making his way back to the vehicle.

"I can't keep checking in for you, Tom," he said over his shoulder. "You know we're supposed to clock in at HQ before heading out. Christ, you've been doing this for twenty-five years. This is the last time. What do you get up to in that flat of yours anyway?"

Tom jogged to catch up with his partner and playfully barged his shoulder with a good-natured joviality.

"Nothing interesting, just running late as usual," he said, pulling himself up into the passenger seat. "Come on then, let's do what we do."

Mike started the engine and pulled out steadily into the night traffic.

CHAPTER EIGHT

It had taken Ethan a little longer than he thought to organise adequate cover of his lectures. He never wanted his students to suffer when he was called upon to help with a live investigation, but it was also something he could never turn down, in spite of his feeble attempts at protest. The attraction of putting his skills to the test against another still far outshone the attraction of seeing students progress into the world. After taking care of work he had spent the day with his daughter, Caitlin, and told her how she would be spending time with Nana as he went off to catch the bad men. They had gone to the park, spending time on the swings and the see-saw, Ethan enjoying watching his little girl being just that. They then watched *Finding Nemo* for the umpteenth time. Caitlin had laughed at all the same moments as the previous viewings, amazed at the thought of an underwater world, and asking questions on sea turtles in machine-gun fashion until it was time for her to go to bed, climbing the stairs and mimicking the seagulls.

"Mine, mine, mine," she said, giggling.

"You know what?" Ethan asked as he pulled her duvet tight around her and her surrounding toys.

"Love you most," she replied quickly, melting Ethan there and then, as she did every time she replied in her cheeky tone.

With Caitlin tucked up, Ethan loaded his cases into the car ready for the short journey into London. She had grown so fast, and was the image of her mother, with the sassy tongue to match. If she was like this now, how would he cope when she hit her teens and boys started complicating things further? It was something he hoped to put off for as long as possible. And if things got really tough, well then there was always Nana to step in and save the day.

The journey down had been pleasantly uneventful with good weather, a lack of traffic and the soothing sound of Zac Brown and his band seeing him all the way to the station where he was to catch up with Tony Meadows and DI Swift. It was there that Abbey had timidly mooted the idea that he could stay in the spare room at hers, a small two-bed house on the outskirts of Golders Green. It made no difference to him where he stayed and a little company would certainly beat a plastic kettle and fourteen-inch TV that a B&B would provide, although he was very aware that he was perhaps staring at Abbey a little more than he should be doing. Meadows was in complete favour as it would save monies from his precious budget and he made it clear that DI Swift would be receiving no more than a thank you and maybe a drink on the next social visit to the pub. Having accepted the offer, he had followed DI Swift's Fiat Punto back north to Golders Green and after parking up, made his way to the terraced property, admiring the presentation of the small cul-de-sac which was home to no more than twenty houses. Each one intrinsically the same, yet with minor nuances of change, allowing them and their owners to stand independently proud.

Following Abbey through the front door, Ethan noticed how the décor and general upkeep of the house kept in step with the close outside. If it were being described in a magazine or by a visiting American it would no doubt be referred to as quaint. Everything had its place. Ornaments adorned shelves and the phone sat neatly on a side table with small pad and pen aligned next to it. Floral wallpaper climbed from the entrance hall up the stairs, and looking through to the kitchen, the wooden worktops and cupboard doors gave an air of farmhouse to the property. For someone so young, the house held a traditional atmosphere about it, a lived-in feel. Abbey walked past the phone, glancing down to check for any incoming messages before hanging her keys on the wooden rail next to an understairs cupboard.

"Upstairs, second door on your left. Drop your stuff and make yourself at home. *Mi casa es su casa*," she said with a smile.

Ethan smiled back and made his way up the steep staircase looking at the photos hung on the wall as he did. An elderly lady, always smiling, in numerous pictures with a little girl, presumably Abbey, right through to her passing out parade. A look of joy and pride evident in each and every photograph.

The room looked as if it had been lifted from an earlier time. White dresser, five-drawer chest and wardrobe along with the textured wallpaper and a hanging chandelier fitting providing the light to the room. The window looked out onto the cul-de-sac, currently showing no signs of activity, with the small grass area forebodingly warning off any fun with its no ball games sign. Ethan tried to remember if those signs even existed when he was a child. Countless evenings had been lost to the football matches played out on the local common, running their course until darkness effectively blew the final whistle. He and his friends content with the twenty-something-each draw that had been played out. Maybe those signs were why the local shops had their nightly visitors take up residence. Ethan rested his case and holdall on the floor by the dresser before sitting on the bed and checking the mattress instinctively as if he were in a guest house somewhere. Abbey called up as Ethan looked over the layout of the rest of the upstairs, locating the airing cupboard and bathroom which left only one other room. Presuming that it could only be Abbey's, he made his way toward the stairs.

"So what do you want for dinner?" she called from the kitchen.

Ethan, making his way down, raised his voice to be heard. "A roof and home cooking. I could get used to this," he said with a quiet chuckle.

Abbey met him at the bottom of the stairs with a leaflet in either hand, both eyebrows raised.

"Indian or Chinese?" she asked.

Ethan's smile grew as he pondered the decision.

Thirty minutes later they were sat at the breakfast bar in the kitchen, dishing up noodles and sweet and sour chicken out of the silver trays acting sufficiently as short-term Thermoses. Abbey had poured two small glasses of white wine, and after clearing away all the paper and card remains, sat down and offered a clink of glasses with the tilt of her head.

"Welcome," she toasted, "to catching a killer."

"If that's what he is?" he said, bumping glasses before replacing it on the surface untouched. "Sadly, it now seems that we are waiting for his next move. Nothing at all while I was away?" he continued.

"Nope. Just more people who didn't see or hear anything. And a dead end on all the blood samples taken. This one doesn't want to be caught does he?" she said.

"They seldom do. This one seems to be more careful though, for now at least," Ethan agreed. "He'll have enough of our attention soon. What about you? I pictured you in somewhere a little more… modern," he continued, changing the mood.

Abbey sniggered, and held her hands out, shrugging her shoulders.

"What can I say? I'm still my gran's little girl, and this will always be her house," she said, shovelling a forkful of noodles into her mouth. "Gran raised me. My mum died in labour, and who knows who my dad was or is? She passed away a few years ago, and I guess I like the house giving the feel that she's still here."

"Nothing wrong with that," Ethan cut in. "Never forget those that were important just because we can't see them each and every day."

"Uh-huh," Abbey agreed, continuing to eat. She went to say something further but noticed that Ethan was already lifting himself from the table.

"I think I'll call it a night if that's okay? It's been a long day, and who knows what tomorrow will bring." His voice was much quieter than it had been previously. "Night."

"Night," Abbey managed through a mouthful of chow mein.

Is it all worth it though? he thought as he slowly climbed the stairs, the pictures summoning memories of time spent with his own family.

CHAPTER NINE

Danny's hand shook as he reached for the payphone and lifted it to his ear, calming his breathing and trying to reduce his heart rate as he prepared to speak, every word typed out on the piece of paper resting upon the metal shelf in the booth. The shaking was not from fear, however, it was raw adrenaline coursing through his body. He felt exhilarated, alive, and powerful. It was everything he had been promised. And how easy it had been, far easier than finding a public payphone. *Does Tutor know what decade we are living in?* Danny thought to himself.

He'd picked her up as he had been instructed; peruse and select, put them at ease. She thought he was just another John, not even the luxury of a car, wonderful. No doubt they'd be walking to her place, or some dingy alleyway before she got her money. She had hoped, as ever, for the comfort and warmth of a hotel. That was becoming rarer and rarer these days. Maybe even the luxury of a bath afterwards. Was it too much to ask to be treated with some level of dignity? But what option did she have? They had the money and she needed it. It was basic economics in her mind, supply and demand. When you had a habit to feed and no one there to offer a helping hand, she knew you did what was necessary.

"So what you after, mister?" she asked, taking his hand and placing it on her chest.

Danny smiled kindly, picturing someone else entirely.

"Just you, good-looking." He took her hand and they started to walk the street, him smiling softly to put her at ease. With the exception of her attire they could be mistaken for a young couple in the wrong part of town. The streetlights had been smashed in the majority, leaving only a handful of low-emitting amber glows to highlight the shadows of both the literal and metaphoric rats that scurried in and out of the dark. Coming out into the open only when necessary to complete the various transactions available dependent on their wares.

"You must be cold?" he asked. "I've got a place local, we can go there and make you more comfortable," he offered.

A real gentleman, she thought. *This guy may even tip. Still, basic economics, get the price set. That takes all complication out of the way.*

"How long you want me for, mister?"

"Forever," he retorted, "don't worry about time. Money won't be an issue."

"Really?" she said with a mischievous smile. "Then you could be in for a night you'll never forget," she continued playfully.

A thought passed across Danny's face until he composed himself and looked deep into her brown eyes.

"Let's hope so," he said, squeezing her hand fondly.

They walked for a further ten minutes, working their way out of the deprived back streets into a more affluent neighbourhood entirely. The smile on her face growing as she took in the houses and cars that adorned every driveway. He knew he had to make it appear as if he knew exactly where he was going. Like he belonged there. He had committed the address to memory and walked with a purposeful stride, leading her gently, making her feel wanted and creating a sense of trust. He stopped suddenly outside a large gate protecting the entrance path to an Edwardian townhouse.

"Here we are," he said, opening the gate as quietly as possible.

"Nice digs," she countered, following him up the pathway.

He made sure to tread carefully, never leaving the path.

"Only thing is we need to go in the back. Got some work being done in the hallway."

As he led her down the side alley he fought hard to control his breathing, feeling the sweat of excitement and anticipation forcing its way through his skin, making him feel flush. He was now completely in the hands of Tutor. Closing his eyes, he lifted the latch of the back gate, the click of success made his heart lift as he stepped onto the patio. Turning his attention to the back door on his left, he pushed the handle down steadily and sighed with relief as he pulled the door towards him, gesturing for her to move into the dark of the room before them.

She walked uneasily into the dark, for the first time a sense of apprehension about her.

"You not have any lights in this place?" she asked, trying to hold a confidence in her voice that wasn't really there.

"Of course," he said soothingly. "Far side of the room on the left."

As she moved cautiously across the floor, her heels clicking loudly on the tiles, Danny shuffled around the edge of the units, reaching down and finding the crowbar and arm sling that he already knew would be in place. *Authenticity is key, he recalled.* He had never needed to question his trust of Tutor. He had done all he promised, and now so would Danny.

As the lights flicked on, she turned round with a look of relief and a relaxed smile, taking in her surroundings.

"Nice digs indeed."

She moved forward, reaching for his belt, biting into her lower lip.

Her attempts at sultry changed dramatically as she looked down and saw the hooked iron shaft. A look of terror as her eyes widened, taking in the contorted menace on her gentlemanly John's face, scrambling backwards, with every part of her body flailing hastily without actually getting anywhere fast.

"Forever, Susan," he said softly.

The phone rang at the other end. *Surely the pick-up time should be quicker than this,* he thought.

"Police, emergency."

He breathed deeply. No emotion, that was the instruction.

"I've gone and done it again," he said, clearly and dispassionately.

CHAPTER TEN

Ethan knew the scene would be different on this occasion. He and Abbey would be able to see the victim in place and get a full feel of the last thing the killer had seen before his departure. As he climbed out of the car he noticed Abbey glancing up at the size of the houses, the brief moment of a daydream coming home to this every day fleeting across her face.

"Nice place," he said, bringing her back to the grave reality.

She nodded toward a *For Sale* sign pinned to the surrounding wall, taking another moment of imagination as she strode past him and up the pathway.

"Yours if you want it? May even get a discount now!" she called.

Ethan jogged to catch up as they headed down the narrow alleyway to the back of the house, both pausing briefly before stepping through the back door.

The kitchen was a large square room with small multicoloured tiles reaching from work surface to beech-effect units, cold ceramic tiles on the floor, ivory in colour until they met within touching distance of the victim where they were stained red. Bruised, battered and bludgeoned to death, mass contusions hiding what appeared to have once been a pretty face, and a rope taut around her throat.

"You sure this is one of ours?" Ethan asked, trying to take in the scene and relate it to anything from memory.

"Who knows? I know it's on our patch though," Abbey said as she made her way carefully around the body, toward the glass dining-room table. "What do you suppose this is then?" she posed, lifting up what appeared to be an arm sling with the end of her pen.

Ethan breathed a heavy sigh as he realised it was indeed their man. Rubbing the back of his neck, he looked from the body back to Abbey.

"Ted Bundy," he said solemnly. "He lured his victims by feigning injury. He gained their trust by appearing weak. Look at our girl though. Does she look like trust is a big part of her make-up?"

"There is a lot of make-up," she replied dryly, moving in to take a closer look. "She's a working girl. Seeing this place, probably thought she'd hit the jackpot. Instead, she became a piñata."

"And worse I'd presume. Seeing how authenticity seems to be of such high priority. That being the case, she'll have been raped too," Ethan said.

Abbey lifted the woman's skirt gently, closing her eyes and putting her hand over her mouth as she re-laid the garment and climbed unsteadily to her feet.

"You can tell the SOCO guys it's all theirs. And that they had better find something for us this time." Abbey walked past Ethan without pause, retching as she went in search of fresh air.

Leaning against the car, Ethan could see that Abbey was still venting as she paced the pavement from one end of the car to the other.

"You know they won't find anything," he said.

"You don't know that," she snapped, stopping abruptly in front of him. "We don't know, until we know."

"I do, and so do you," he said calmly. "We may get something from the autopsy, but even that's unlikely."

"We need something. Did you see what he did to her? Did you? How can you show brutality like that and not leave anything behind?"

"Planning," Ethan replied, "none of this is off the cuff. It's brutal, but it's planned. And methodically so."

Amongst the activity of all the bodies coming and going from the front gate, a stern-looking woman was making her way toward Ethan and Abbey, holding her son's hand, ensuring he keep up with her imposed pace. As she neared her target she pulled her arm forward sharply, thrusting the teenage boy in front of them.

"Go on then, tell them," she snapped, pushing him in the back as a prompt.

The boy shuffled on the spot, staring down at his untied laces, hands in pockets, groaning as if hard done by.

"Tell them," she prompted again.

"I might have seen someone," he mumbled, "last night I mean."

Abbey looked at Ethan, her vitality reignited.

"Ma'am," she said to the woman softly, "I don't think we need to go to the station, but maybe we could go inside? How about a cup of tea? That all right with you?" she asked, lifting the boy's chin with her finger to make eye contact.

Elizabeth Carrington brought the tea through on a silver tray, placing it gently on the nest of oak tables in the middle of the lounge. Having been used to drinks from a vending machine, receiving tea from a Wedgwood pot in Fortnum & Mason china cups was a whole new experience for DI Swift. The room looked out onto the street and had an air of money that had matched the feeling when walking in through the hallway. Large paintings hung on the three main walls, creating a dark overhanging gloom to the room, even though the sun shone brightly through the large bay window, reflecting off the shiny thread within the Indian rug that filled the floorspace. *This room is worth more than my house*, Abbey thought as she took the tea with a pleasant smile. Elizabeth smiled momentarily, before shooting a look at her son, letting him know that the pleasantries were not yet extended to him.

"Matthew," she instructed, taking a seat herself.

Abbey looked over toward Ethan who nodded for her to take the lead with the boy. She shuffled forward to sit on the edge of the sofa, hands between her knees, trying to put Matthew at ease.

"Matthew, what did you see last night? Were you looking out of this window?"

"No, he wasn't," Elizabeth said suddenly. "If your father knew…"

"Mum," Matthew groaned, "I said I'm sorry."

"You're always sorry, Matthew."

"Mrs Carrington, if we could just find out what he saw," Ethan asked kindly.

"So where were you?" Abbey asked, regaining control of the conversation, realising that any shred of information was better than what they had at present.

"In the alleyway at the end of the road… With my mates," he began sheepishly. "We were…"

"Smoking, they were smoking again," Elizabeth interrupted, shaking her head in disgust.

Abbey raised a hand sharply, preventing Elizabeth from continuing in her mini-tirade against her son. Matthew nodded dolefully.

"He walked past the alleyway with the prostitute. I didn't even know that's what she was. But Neville seemed pretty confident, said you could tell by the way she was dressed. We watched them go off to the house, which seemed strange as it was up for sale, and I thought they were away on holiday. But we just thought it was funny," he said, speaking quicker and quicker. "Anyway, he walks past us again, about forty-five minutes later, on his own, whistling and carrying a duck's head. We just watched him go and started cracking up. Wasn't until this morning, when all you lot turned up, that it seemed important."

"A duck's head?" Ethan queried with raised eyebrows.

"Appeared that way to us," he said, shrugging.

"So what did he look like?" Abbey asked. "Anything distinguishable from everyone else? Different," she said, correcting herself.

"Not really. He was just a normal guy. Normal height, brown hair… I think, but it was so dark, and we were trying not to be seen. Mid-twenties maybe."

"You're sure," Ethan said sharply.

"I guess," Matthew said. "Certainly wasn't some old dude."

Ethan and Abbey left Matthew in the threatening company of his mother as she pondered whether to let her husband in on their son's antics. He would be so ashamed, she had explained. "People just don't act like that around here."

"People round here just don't know what their kids get up

to, smoking might be the least of their worries," Abbey had said to Ethan as they walked down the steps, making their way back towards the car.

"Mid-twenties, Doc?" Abbey said with an impish grin. "Don't tell me you were wrong."

"I won't, not yet anyway," Ethan retorted. "So where to now?"

"We need to check in with Meadows, and I want to get people out doing the rounds. A street corner is missing a hooker, someone must have seen her."

The car ride back to the station had been quiet, both going over their individual thought processes with nothing clear enough worthy of sharing. Once back on familiar territory Ethan had excused himself in order to call home and ensure all was well. He hadn't mentioned family up to this point so Abbey decided she wouldn't try and draw that from him at this stage. As she made her way through the corridors in the direction of her office, she passed a young PC in the incident room of the 'copycat killer' as he had imaginatively been called throughout the station, and clicked her fingers as she walked past.

"Come on then, if you want something more interesting than phone monitoring?"

As she settled into a chair behind her desk, resting her chin on her hands, she looked up at a young recruit lingering in her doorway.

"So...?" she queried.

"Johnson, ma'am. You asked for me. Well, someone. To help with tonight?"

"Okay, Johnson, cancel any plans you had, you're gonna be

hitting the town. We'll pair you with Vice for the evening. You'll like them, and they'll make sure you stay in line when you get to speak to all the pretty little ladies of the night."

PC Johnson reddened slightly, looking around the tiny office.

"Go, Johnson, go get some sleep, and be ready for Vice this evening. You'll be back here for eleven. Clear?"

"Ma'am," Johnson acknowledged with a nod.

Ethan was always amazed at the buzz of activity around a station at any given time of the day. Whether there were high-profile cases as there was presently or just the day-to-day coming and going of officers clocking in and out on a rotating cycle, the place bustled with an ever-present commotion. He made his way to Abbey's office in a relaxed mood having heard Caitlin's laugh and all about the planets she'd learned about that day at school. She had been excited on the phone after finding out her best friend Jenny would be going to the same junior school in September. *Junior school,* he thought, *that's when the troubles will begin.* His little girl would be introduced to everything that scared Elizabeth Carrington so much. He just hoped she would be strong enough to resist temptation. He had made his way through the station before he realised that he was stood at Abbey's door with her looking intensely at the computer screen in front of her.

"Hey, you," he said, pulling her from her thoughts.

"Did you know," she said, "that I put *copycat killings* into Google news and the first entry I got was our case? How did that get on there? How? We haven't released any of the details."

"Interest in the macabre, I guess. Only takes one individual to pass on what they know. How do the papers get any of their information?"

"Money and a lack of integrity," Abbey said with disdain. "Anyway, I've been looking at infamous killers that may provide inspiration. The list is endless. How are we supposed to second-guess this freak?"

"It's dismissive to label him a freak, Abbey. He'll blend into society and have an above-average intelligence at worst. And sadly, we can't second-guess. We have to wait for a mistake," Ethan said.

"Well, that's bullshit. You're saying we have to sit around waiting for him to act out his next little fantasy and hope he gets it wrong? No, he's already made a mistake, we just need to find it."

A double tap on the already open door broke the tension of silence in the room as Robbie from the front desk popped his head into the office.

"Hi, Abbey, Meadows is back in, but he's on the warpath. Just been for his blood donation appointment supporting the chief super's drive of emergency services supporting each other. Apparently it took them four attempts to find a vein," he said with a chortle.

"Perfect," Abbey snorted as she put her head in her hands.

"That's it," Ethan exclaimed as he turned and sprinted from the room.

His heart pounded so hard he thought it was going to burst from his chest as he lengthened his stride racing along the corridor. This is why he had come back when asked. No classroom, or student, could provide this level of exuberance, of accomplishment. Sidestepping obstacles and individuals he threw all his weight into the door of the incident room, bursting into the empty space beyond. As his lungs gasped for air, his eyes scanned the board feverishly for the words he knew were in the jumble of letters somewhere.

Abbey caught up with Ethan in the incident room, a marker

in his hand, beaming from ear to ear. He had circled the words *'multi bloods'* under the photo of the first victim and tapped the board furiously.

"What?" she huffed, trying to catch her breath.

"The bloods, *multiple contributors* Meadows said," he panted then paused, waiting for Abbey to interrupt, but she shook her head in wonder.

"And?"

Sighing, he continued. "What if he had said *multiple donors?* No other reported crime scenes, no criminal records against any of the blood tested. It was all given voluntarily, Abbey, the blood was donated."

"Son of a bitch, he's a medicine man," she said.

CHAPTER ELEVEN

"Come on, Doc, my treat," Abbey enthused, "plus you'll want to hear the results of the autopsy won't you?"

"Hmm, and that is happening in here is it?" Ethan asked.

The noise emanating from within could've been from any pub or bar in the city, and while Ethan couldn't say why, he knew instinctively this was solely for people on the job.

"It is when the exam is on a Thursday," Abbey said, pushing open the oak doors to The Highwayman.

"How apt," Ethan said, looking up at the hanging pub sign depicting a man in a mask and a swag bag, following Abbey into the throng of people blocking their way to the bar.

"We like it," Abbey called, already making her way through the masses having caught sight of Lucy, jostling at the bar to order a drink.

The pub appeared to have been recently redecorated in modern trend with the popular quiz machines filling every recess in order to increase turnover. An attempt maybe to attract new customers, which given its location was always going to prove unlikely. Like a lot of pubs, once they had become a copper's place, then no amount of superficial marketing was going to change that.

"Here we are then," Lucy said, setting the drinks down on the sticky surface of the only empty table in the place.

"It always this busy in here?" Ethan asked, taking a long sip of his drink.

"Every Thursday," Abbey said. "Where else we gonna go?"

"Why Thursday?" Ethan asked.

"Why not?" Abbey said as if the question made no sense to her.

"I suppose you want all the grisly details, Ethan, see if we can improve on your epiphany moment earlier today?" Lucy ribbed, smirking at her friend who had obviously relayed his little revelation from the incident room.

Blushing a little, Ethan tilted his head in mock recognition and a cue for Lucy to explain her day's findings.

"She was mid to late twenties, sexually active, not surprising if I'm right on her occupation."

"You will be," Abbey chipped in.

"Cause of death was strangulation, though there were multiple strikes to the head with a blunt instrument. A bar of some sort maybe? Best guess is that she was knocked unconscious and then strangled. And given that you're looking at the copycat guy, I'm sure you'll already know she was raped post mortem?"

"Small mercies at least that it was post mortem," Ethan offered.

"Not by a person though. A lot of brutality went into the act, but it was done with a foreign object," she surmised.

"A duck's head," Abbey mumbled with a quizzical look.

"That could be anything," Ethan countered. "Who knows what they really saw. Or what they were smoking. We've got underage kids, hidden in the shadows, watching someone walk by without a care in the world apparently. We already know they've got his age wrong," he said insolently.

"Have they?" Abbey asked. "Drinks?" she called over her shoulder, already making her way back to the bar.

Lucy was getting up from the table, looking off into a distance far beyond the solid wall that was actually blocking her way.

"You get the drinks," she said, looking at her friend. "Don't go anywhere though. I'll be back in less than an hour."

"Where you going, Luce?" Abbey called as her friend disappeared amongst the crowd.

"To get me one of those epiphanies," she shouted back.

Abbey arrived back at the table with another three drinks, Ethan pointing at himself, then Abbey, then pausing at the empty chair.

"She can catch up," Abbey said nonchalantly, taking her seat. "Wanna play twenty questions?" she asked.

"Why not?" Ethan replied, taking a sip of his drink.

"Cool. What's your favourite colour?"

"Excuse me?"

"Your favourite colour. It's an easy one to start with. You know, for a professor, sometimes you're not that bright!"

"I'm not sure you understand the concept."

"Sure I do. I asked if you wanted to play twenty questions. You said yes. And now I'm going to ask you twenty questions. Not sure how you thought this game would work?"

"Fine, fine," he conceded, "fire at will."

"Colour," Abbey repeated.

"Red."

"Film?"

"*Rounders*, Matt Damon and Edward Norton."

"I know who's in it," she snapped. "Author?"

Ethan exhaled slowly, frowning.

"Ludlum," he said, nodding.

"Real favourite author?"

"Rowling," Ethan conceded with a grin.

"Thank you, band?"

"Thunder."

"Pardon? I asked for your favourite band. You appear to have given me your favourite type of weather."

"One and the same I'm afraid."

"Uh-huh. Well, do expand. What are they? Some sort of thrash metal?"

"No. They're more soft rock. Think Bryan Adams meets Bon Jovi."

"Sounds like the start of a really bad joke," Abbey said. "So you like rock music?"

"Country really, I just grew up with Thunder."

"Oh dear God, it gets worse."

"Come on, next question," Ethan demanded.

"Erm, your favourite..."

"Oh dear, Swift. I do hope your interrogations are better than this. Out of questions at number four. Disappointing," Ethan said, shaking his head.

"No, I've plenty, favourite weather." She grinned.

"Desperate," Ethan said, lifting himself from the table. "Want some food on my way back?"

"Just make it three more," she said.

"But we haven't even touched these yet."

"And Lucy said she'd be a while. Plus it's..."

"Thursday," Ethan interjected as he made his way from the table.

It was an hour and a quarter before Lucy re-entered the pub, which had lost some of its patrons but none of the vibrancy from earlier on. Making her way back to the table she saw Ethan and Abbey nursing two nearly drained glasses and a group of four untouched, pushed to one side.

"Hey," Abbey said, "bought you one every time we got a round in." She gestured proudly.

Ethan waved an acknowledging arm, looking all the worse for the drinks already consumed.

"Thanks," Lucy said, a little perplexed by how they had managed to drink so much in the short space of time she had been gone.

Standing with her arms behind her back and an impudent expression, Ethan and Abbey straightened themselves up with an inquiring look toward the pathologist.

"Why you looking so pleased with yourself?" Abbey asked suspiciously.

Lucy's smile grew broader as she brought her hands into view holding a speculum.

"What would you say that was?" Lucy asked Ethan directly, squeezing a lever to make the two prongs open and close animatedly.

"A duck's head," Ethan said in astonishment.

"As would the majority of men, and young boys," Lucy debated, raising her eyebrows.

"I wouldn't, I'd say they are a bloody torture instrument," Abbey butted in. "Genius."

As Abbey hurriedly made her way across the bar to the restrooms, Lucy sat down at the table shaking her head, making a start on the first of her drinks.

"To epiphanies," she said to Ethan, offering her glass in a congratulatory toast.

CHAPTER TWELVE

Slash: You don't know what it feels like, Clown. You trying to step into your hero's shoes?
Clown: Believe what you want, Slash, but until you've decided whether someone lives or dies, then keep your petty thoughts to yourself.

The conversation had started well before he got in from his shift, and sadly it was still at full pace when Tom had finally been able to log on to the forum. Apparently, he had misjudged his little apprentice. Living up to his user pseudonym fully, he had been running his mouth to all and sundry. Ties would have to be cut, quickly and painlessly. If he was so vocal on the forum, it would only be a matter of time before he started prattling away in the real world. And that was a situation that could never be allowed to occur. Had he not stressed the absoluteness of anonymity clearly enough? Had their shared pleasure not been theirs alone? He had been disappointed by others before, but never by someone singled out by his own critique. This was as much a failing of his own, more so even, as it was his students.

He pulled his chair forward at such a rate his body slammed into the desk, shaking the monitor and surrounding hardware. His nostrils flared as his pupils narrowed, clenching his teeth so hard he could feel his jaw fighting against its own applied pressure. He stared blankly at the screen, all the text congealing to form a black mass in front of him as he slowed his own bodily rhythms, in through the nose, out through the mouth. In through the nose, out through the mouth.

Not this time, he thought as the words came back into focus and his breathing quickened once more.

He punched the keys furiously, every word given as much venom as he could muster. Clown would be in no doubt as to the sentiment, there would be no lack of translation in this message, and no way could it be misconstrued. As if attempting to push his finger completely through the mouse, he sent the private message, pushed himself away from the desk and stormed from the room, punching the door as he made his way to the bathroom.

Less than a mile away Danny Jemson was happily tapping away at his terminal. Tutor had been right. He still felt a burning within from his activities the night before. How could he describe how he felt? Words escaped him as he tried to explain. He physically shook with the memory, reliving every moment of the greatest night of his life. The whore had been perfect. No one would miss her. Almost as good as the real thing. She'd be sorted soon enough though. He just had to convince Tutor that she was deserving of being their next sacrifice. He shivered suddenly, every muscle in his body tensing, closing his eyes, imagining how he could hold her fate in his hands. A sadistic smile broke out as he allowed his imagination to wander. All he wanted was for Tutor to contact him and relieve his mounting yearning. The anticipation was building inside him. He didn't think he could contain his new urges for much longer.

The sound of a laughing clown grabbed his attention back in reality, his moniker for the private message. Danny's satanic leer reappeared as his eyes flickered with excitement. He could already feel himself pulling the trigger, thrusting the knife or tightening the rope.

Danny's jaw dropped as he read the text in front of him. Swallowing hard, trying to breathe, he struggled to convince himself that Tutor could never find him, despite what the message relayed. His hands trembled over the keys, positioning them to type then retracting his hands once more, re-reading the poison on his screen. Every part of him wanted to escape to his bed, wrap himself up from the world and hide, but he found himself captivated by the screen, knees drawn up to his chest and tears running down his face.

Tom paced his apartment, naked, air-drying, the bath having soothed away most of the anger that had arisen within him. Moving through to the kitchen he poured himself a tall glass of milk and walked the apartment until he had drained the milk in full, composing himself to return to the forum. He shook his head as he moved into the study, looking at the damage to the door, before seating himself gently at the desk.

"No emotion," he reprimanded himself aloud.

He quickly scanned the chat of the last hour or so. No sign of Clown. A satisfying nod as he pulled the keyboard forward. He stretched his arms out in front of him and cracked his knuckles, noticing that the site's newest contributor was once again logged in.

B&B: I just want to protect us. I don't admire killers. I thought someone on here could tell me how to sort real problems. You're all sick.
 Jags: So why stick around? You and Bulldog are the sick ones. You lurk. You're always on here, but always in the background. The quiet ones are the most dangerous. Isn't that what they say? Ha Ha Ha.
 Sudo: You know you love it, B&B. Nothing wrong with wanting rid of family. They give you more reason than most.
 Jags: Come on, B&B, how you want to do him? Nice and slow, painful? Gotta make 'em suffer.
 B&B: I don't know how, that's what I need to know. I don't care if he suffers, I just want him to leave us alone. If none of you can help then I don't need you.

Tom started to type, quickly, proofreading as he did so. It would only be a small window of opportunity between the young man's threat to log out forever and him actually doing so.

Private Message
 From:Tutor
 To:B&B
 Ref:Hitchcock
 You don't have to feel helpless. Ignore the imbeciles. I can help. If you really want to protect your mother? We can help each other.

Tom leaned back, resting his hands on top of his head, and hoped he had caught the attention of what appeared to be a desperately troubled individual.

The reply came back in a private chat room.

B&B: How can you help? Why would you?
Tutor: Have you ever seen Strangers on a Train?
B&B: I know of the book.

CHAPTER THIRTEEN

The mobile phone vibrated on the nightstand, just out of Abbey's reach. Every pulsation boring like a pneumatic drill through her skull. Lifting her neck slightly, wincing at the pain and groaning as she attempted to open her eyes, she fumbled for the phone, knocking it to the floor, crashing down with the sound of an imploded building.

"Fuck it," she husked, her mouth as dry as a dirt track.

Forcing her eyes open she reached down, grabbing the phone.

"What?" she managed in no more than a whisper, the word getting caught in her throat halfway out.

"Morning, ma'am," answered a perky PC Johnson, "got someone to see you down the station," he continued, pleased with himself.

Abbey bolted up in bed, her head some seconds behind the rest of her body.

"She'll be in interview room three, when you're in a suitable state to see her," he taunted.

"Thirty minutes," she said, hanging up. Pulling the duvet up to bury her face she growled into the lining before making her way to the shower, knocking hard on Ethan's door until a suitable grunt of recognition was heard.

"Up," she called.

Abbey burst through the doors of the station, tangled wet hair flying behind her as she scanned the reception area for the large frame of PC Johnson. He caught her eye first and shook his head, subduing a smirk and holding up three fingers. Abbey grabbed Ethan trailing in behind her, eyes closed with a hand over his face, pulling him toward the corridor leading to the interview rooms. The corridor was empty, allowing them some recovery time, automatically slowing their walk, breathing deeply as they closed in on room three halfway down.

"Ready for this?" Abbey asked.

"Not really, my head is spinning. Not a great impression to give, is it?"

"Pfft, she sees worse than you on a nightly basis. Just don't throw up," Abbey said with a wicked smile, before pressing down on the door handle.

The room was sanitary, devoid of feeling or welcome, with just a single table in the middle, dimly lit by the murky daylight forcing its way through the solitary window, two chairs on either side. A camera perched intrudingly in the corner, a witness to every movement or statement made for permanent record. Ethan shuddered as they entered, glancing around the room uncomfortably, ignoring the ageing woman on one side of the table.

"Hey, sugar, you need me to help you relax?" the woman said.

"Now, now, Sharon, play nice," Abbey rebutted, "Ethan, Sharon, Sharon, Ethan Marshall."

"A pleasure," Sharon said as Ethan smiled politely, raising a hand.

"Me and Sharon go way back. Helped us cut down on the number of local pimps when I was working vice," Abbey continued. "I hear you want to give us a hand again?"

"A hand's twenty-five quid, darling, less your Met discount of course."

"Always thinking of others," Abbey retorted.

"I like to do what I can. I'm a giver, what can I say?" Sharon said, glancing at Ethan.

"I'm sure that's appreciated by your... clients, but we're more interested in what you did or didn't see the night one of you girls chose the wrong John," Ethan snapped. "Or you can continue with your inane innuendos. Either you're here to help or you're not?"

Sharon started to tap an unlit cigarette on the table, swallowed and looked toward Abbey. Abbey turned to look out of the window, losing herself to the coming and going officers on the pavement outside, removing herself from the interview process.

"Who's to say it's not you next time?" Ethan posed, softening his tone. "All we want is to get this guy off the streets, so please, just tell us what you saw."

Sharon dropped her eyes to the tabletop, continuing to tap the cigarette butt.

"Smartly dressed, looked like he'd made an effort, you know. Somewhere in his twenties. Not your usual punter. We normally see the older types, not getting it at home anymore, or at least not the way they want it," she said dryly. "Anyway, Lisa was the lucky pick, or so we thought."

"And?" Ethan probed.

"And nothing, they went off to do whatever shit he wanted to do to her. Didn't see her again, did we?" Sharon finished.

"Look, honey," she said, leaning forward over the table, "I was told you see something, you come in tomorrow, or, you get done for soliciting and maybe spend the night. I can't afford to lose that kind of money."

"Okay," Abbey interrupted as Ethan shook his head. "Sharon, out, and don't be lighting that until you're out of the station."

"Jesus. You try and do your civic duty..."

Sharon pulled herself to her feet, tutted and strode from the room.

"And be careful," Abbey shouted after her.

The room fell into silence as the door clicked shut. Ethan stared at the table, running his hands through his hair and across the stubble on his face.

"There's a side to you we haven't seen before, Doc. You all right?"

Ethan stood and started to pace the room, clasping his hands together and chewing on his thumbs.

"I'm just tired, and being given help by someone who knows nothing isn't helpful. This guy is getting ready to make his next move and we still have no idea where it might be or who he is."

"Don't beat yourself up, Doc, we'll get there. Like you said, we may need to be patient," Abbey said encouragingly, "and we know more than we did. Both witnesses put him in his twenties, and we work on him being a medical guy."

Ethan quickened his stride, rubbing his hands back over his face, shaking his head. His body ached from head to toe. All he wanted to do was crawl back to bed and lose consciousness to sleep with the aid of some paracetamol. But he knew sleep would not come easy now. Not until progress was being made. It was a trait he wished he could rid himself of, but once immersed, his active mind was the catalyst for insomnia.

"If he's in his twenties, then this isn't our guy. How many

doctors do you know still in their early twenties?" Ethan asked. "Something isn't right with what we have, it just doesn't sit right."

Abbey moved over and put a hand on Ethan's shoulder. Taking his hand, she led him over to sit down at the table, seating herself in the chair opposite. Ethan bowed his head to the desktop, eyes closed, rubbing at his temples. Abbey lifted his chin, smiling softly.

"What's really bothering you, Ethan?"

Ethan opened his eyes, biting into his lip, his eyes reddening as he fought the tears forming.

"It's the tiredness, I know it is. I'm being asinine. Going out like we did last night..."

"Yeah," Abbey urged.

"I don't do it," Ethan said, shrugging his shoulders, breathing deeply. "Not for a long time anyway."

Abbey sat silently, placing a hand on top of Ethan's, fighting the temptation to probe further as Ethan gained control and added a little steel back into his voice.

"I haven't been out, not even to a pub of an evening for nearly four years. It's been a case of work, then home to look after Caitlin," Ethan said with a heavy sigh, lifting his head to eye level with Abbey. "Emily, my wife, was killed, because of my work. I take it you know that?"

"I heard, though I don't think you can blame yourself or your work for what happened," Abbey said.

"We'll have to agree to disagree," Ethan said, managing half a smile. "Yet I can't leave it alone. I keep letting myself get drawn back in. And the longer we go without stopping him, the longer I'm away from Caitlin, when I should be putting her first," he concluded.

"It's something we have to do, Doc. Not really a choice, more an undertaking that makes us what we are. We will catch him though. And for what it's worth, I think your little girl would be proud of her dad. For what he's done and for what he's doing," Abbey said, rising from the table. "Can I ask you a question?" she said softly.

Ethan lifted his head to make eye contact.

"What the hell does asinine mean?"

Ethan laughed aloud.

"Why don't you go home and try and get some sleep, and learn how to handle your drink," she continued with a grin.

CHAPTER FOURTEEN

The IV tube came loose in his hands as they took another sharp corner, sirens wailing, ensuring all those around them should, in theory at least, be roughing their cars onto the paved streets of London accordingly. The number of lives lost to the ignorance of central Londoners was staggering. The statistics would be released annually and reported in shockwaves through the evening news and daily papers, attracting reactions of disgust and a call for change from the public and politicians alike. The only emergency of any magnitude was that of their own little world, picking up the kids from school, making it home in time for dinner. These were things that simply couldn't wait, and certainly not for something as trivial as a punctured lung or profuse bleeding.

"For Christ's sake, keep her steady will you," Tom barked over the din of the ambulance.

Mike shook his head with a heavy sigh as he threw the ambulance left then right to narrowly avoid becoming the meat in a Fiat 500 sandwich. *Young yuppies, bloody tin-pot wagons are everywhere.*

Tom wiped the sweat from his forehead on the thick plastic

of his sleeve, ensuring the blood that covered his gloves never reached his skin as he secured the IV line to the catheter.

"Four minutes out," Mike called, eyes never leaving the obstacle course in front of them.

At least three too late for this one.

Tom leant back into the side panelling of the carriage, craning his neck and stretching his arms out to their full extension, trying to gain some relief from the cramped environment. Tilting his head, he looked into the eyes of the woman in front of him. Still conscious, her eyes were looking for some recognition of hope, that all would be okay. Tom continued to stare unerringly. He had done all he could to save her, but this one was for him now, and he would see it through to its inevitable conclusion with her.

The ambulance pulled up with the gurney ready and waiting as the back doors flew open and seemingly transferred the woman in milliseconds. Mike climbed down from his seat, pulling a pack of cigarettes from his pocket, stretching his neck from side to side as Tom raced out after the hospital staff transporting his patient.

"Tom, we've done our bit," Mike groaned after his partner.

"I need to be there," Tom called back as he ran into the main building.

This is the good bit, I need to see her go.

Danny Jemson sat at his screen re-reading the email that had taken so long to get word perfect. He'd grown in confidence since receiving Tutor's last contact. An empty threat, he had decided. There had been no follow-up. And he had the sanctity of the internet as his cover. How could he know where he lived?

The others on the forum had been right, he was all talk. He was the one who had held life in his hands, not Tutor. All he had done was put some props in place. Any fool could do that. And Tutor would know exactly how he felt. He didn't need him anyway. He was his own man.

A god even, for who else gets to decide who lives or dies?

Danny dug his fingers into the side of the mouse in an attempt to control the trembling as he puffed out his cheeks and approved the sending of his true thoughts.

Tom felt refreshed as he made his way into the apartment. The others had gone for a drink, as usual, in order to relieve the stresses of the day. He had politely declined, as usual, and walked home, the fixated smile of a little boy having received his most wanted Christmas present etched upon his face. She had been a bonus, the beneficial circumstance that would occur on occasion and went hand in hand with his chosen profession. With the high still coursing through his body, it was time to put into effect the greater rush that could only be obtained by constructing the environment where the ending was predetermined.

Having showered and dried off, Tom sat at his computer with a cold glass of milk as the excitement of the day wore off, leaving only his concentration focused on the matter in hand. He was pleased to see that he had received a couple of private messages and clicked on the icon with interest. Tom had left his last message open-ended, a mere suggestion of resolution and an offer of help should the young man want it. It was up to him whether they were to progress together. Though he was in no doubt that the immediate future would pan out exactly as he planned. As he allowed his thoughts to form, seeing the act, imagining the feeling swell inside him, the empowerment within himself and that he had given to someone else, he was brought sharply back to the present as his face contorted with fury taking in the first few lines, not from B&B but someone who should've been smart enough to cut ties when given the opportunity. It was a one-time offer, and now that chance had been passed up.

Classroom asst,

You know my name only because I let you, I am the one who decides when I am finished. You are nothing more than a supplier of materials. It is you who need me, not the other way round. How dare you threaten me when it is I who have looked into death's eyes. You are no more than a hollow voice to me. You hide from your dreams and ask others to achieve what you only fantasise about. You had a chance to be part of this and have run away from that. Coward is too kind a word for you, a pathetic shell of a man. I will continue to go where you are unable.

The Laughing (at you) Clown.

As hatred and rage swelled within him, Tom felt the pressure increase on the glass as it shattered in his hand, tearing at the flesh as he balled it into a fist, a mess of claret and cool milk dripping onto the carpet below.

"Fuck it," he roared, sweeping keyboard, mouse and monitor onto the floor.

CHAPTER FIFTEEN

Superintendent Meadows sat back in his chair, stretching his arm out before him and looking across his desk at Ethan and Abbey for a hint of optimism.

"You've got to give me something," he said, now rubbing his temples. "I take it you've seen the papers?"

"I'd like to know where they get their information," Abbey snapped.

Ethan smiled, looking from Meadows to Abbey.

"Come on, we know where they get their information. And we know how they get it. It's maybe just getting cheaper for them to get it."

"I know how it makes us look," Meadows interjected. "Two murders..."

"We don't know the first was murder," Abbey stated.

"Perfect, so we don't even know what we're investigating. Hardly confidence-inspiring, is it?" Meadows continued.

"Yes we do," Ethan said authoritatively. "We know that one murder has been committed. We know that however tenuous the link, the guy is in the medical industry."

"Or woman," Meadows said, shaking his head.

"No, it's a guy. We've got your people doing rounds of the hospitals. If anything is awry, it'll be found. Your man is of high intelligence, but bodies and blood don't go missing unnoticed. Background checks are being carried out on the first vic. That body is either family or found to serve a purpose. There are too many open queries, Tony. He can't cover everything. It's a matter of when we get the break, not if," Ethan concluded.

"Yeah," Abbey said with a grin toward her superintendent, who raised his eyebrows in return.

"Sir," she corrected, her smile broadening.

"I'm glad you're so confident, Ethan, because now the press has got a hold of this we are going to need to make a move in the right direction, and quickly. The coverage will only worsen should the unthinkable happen."

Ethan shrugged as he walked the perimeter of the office, looking at the sporting pictures adorning the walls, stopping at a picture of an NFL quarterback in mid throw.

"This one's new," Ethan stated.

"Urgh, not you too?" Abbey asked.

"Drew..." Tony began.

"Drew Brees, MVP Superbowl forty-four, thirty-two completions from thirty-nine attempted passes, two hundred and eighty-eight yards total, for two touchdowns," Ethan interrupted.

"Indeed," Meadows replied, tipping an imaginary cap.

"How do you know all that rubbish?" Abbey asked in amazement.

"Two reasons," Meadows began, beating Ethan to the response. "Firstly, our Doc as you call him is as passionate about sport as I am, and secondly, it helps with his hobby," he concluded, making air quotation marks as he did so.

"What's your hobby?"

"Yes, how do you word it again, Ethan?"

"I review sports for financial benefit," Ethan said with a smile.

"Didn't have you as a gambler, Doc."

"I try to remove as much of the gamble element as I can. But what can I say? Everyone has their vice."

The lightened mood in the office was pierced by the shrill ring of a phone, causing ripples of movement across the desk surface from the swell of red tape awaiting the superintendent's consideration.

"Just get me something," Meadows pleaded, rummaging for the handset as Abbey and Ethan took their cue to leave.

"Not many get to speak to the guv'nor like that," Abbey said, as they walked the corridor heading back toward the incident room.

"The luxury of being here by invitation I guess," Ethan said. "We've known each other long enough for no offence to be taken. Plus, I'm right, these tracks can't stay hidden for long. It just depends on what happens before we see that first print in the sand."

Walking into the empty incident room, Ethan rested upon the desk nearest the front and tried to take in the sea of information before him on the whiteboard, a frown forming as he looked over the left-hand side of blue marker pen and photos.

"So what are we missing?" Abbey asked, taking the same stance next to him, scanning the identical faces and data in plain view.

"Who wrote in red?" Ethan asked quizzically, walking toward the whiteboard.

"What?" Abbey asked, perplexed, her eyes drawn to where Ethan was now standing.

"We seem to have a reference for a Mr Arthur Green, and a date to go with it," he said, walking over and tapping the whiteboard at the point blue turned to red, 7/9/09 004205.

"A little vague don't you think?" Abbey asked. "I'll get the call put out, shouldn't take long to find the bright spark who thought this was their little secret."

"And while we wait?" Ethan posed.

"We eat," Abbey said with a smile. "Your treat."

The police canteen was a hive of activity with all ranks scrambling for a spare seat. Shift change, those wanting to eat before knocking off and those grabbing something to see them through the evening's work ahead. Title went out of the window when it came to the last available seat or half-decent cut of meat, a level playing field for one and all. Ethan strolled casually over and handed a tray to Abbey, who sighed heavily for effect as she snatched the tray.

"The canteen, you really know how to spoil a girl."

"I may even buy you dessert," Ethan quipped as he made his way down the line looking at the rudimentary selections available. "I want to be here when you get a response to that date and reference."

"All well and good, but we won't be able to do anything until tomorrow anyway," she said. "I will have the chef's special please," she said to the cook, watching him throw a watery fish onto a plate with two large scoopfuls of oven chips. "Beautiful, I've not eaten this well since I was at senior school. You owe me a real meal once we have this sorted, Doc," Abbey continued, readdressing Ethan in mock derision.

Ethan reddened a little, making his way to pay for the meals served up. As the two of them spotted a free table the booming voice of the front-desk clerk echoed across the eating hall.

"Hey, Abbey, turns out it was your boy Johnson. Said he left it for the morning when he was back on. Was going to tell you then. Apparently it's a morgue reference."

"Found to serve a purpose then," Ethan said in little more than whisper, looking up from his tray.

CHAPTER SIXTEEN

Susan Fisher opened the door only ajar, the chain in place, just in case she changed her mind, as she peeked round the cavity, trying hard to give an air of confidence. He stood returning her gaze, one arm resting on the wall, the other supporting a rucksack, continually shifting it back up onto his shoulder.

"Thanks for seeing me," Danny said. "Are the terrible two in?"

Susan tried to stifle a little giggle, pulling the door open as far as the chain would allow.

"No, they're out. They'd think I was mad giving you the time of day. I haven't even told them you were coming over," she said.

Danny nodded, he was convinced it was those two that told her she could do better than him in the first place. That she should be looking for a future and not roughing it for a memory when she was older. He knew she wouldn't tell them he was coming though, still ashamed to be seen with him. That wouldn't be a problem for her for much longer though.

"I do appreciate it, Sue, seeing me that is. And I'm doing

what you said. I'm concentrating all my efforts on one thing. No more flaking through. I think I've found something I really want to do," he said, hoisting the bag up again. "Can I just come in? A chat, nothing more," he continued.

Susan took a deep sigh and smiled kindly as she pushed the door to without closing, fiddling with the chain until it came loose. Opening it wide she gestured for him to come in.

"I'm glad," she said, "I always said you were capable of things others weren't."

How true, Danny thought as he made his way through to the lounge of her shared apartment.

Across town, a boy of no more than fifteen made his way out of the Seven Sisters underground station, head down, concentrating hard on the piece of paper held tightly in both hands. As the last great surge of commuters made their way home from their long office hours, Ben Davies didn't even notice as he split a group of highly paid professionals, bemoaning his lack of respect or acknowledgement of their presence as they were forced to move aside from his chosen pathway from which he would not deviate. Fingers turning white as he increased the pressure on the paper, Ben wiped at the tears streaming silently from his eyes. Taking in the directions for the umpteenth time, he lengthened his stride and quickened the pace. The sooner this was over, the sooner he and his mum would be safe.

Susan stretched out, flicking her wrist so she could look at the time on her watch, stifling a yawn.

"Another drink?" Danny asked through gritted teeth.

"I'm actually feeling a little tired, Danny. It has been nice seeing you again though."

Danny shook his head in bewilderment. "So nice you want me gone before your bitch friends come back," he snarled, grabbing at the zip on the bag by his feet to make an opening before standing abruptly and throwing it over his shoulder. Susan dropped her gaze to the floor, shifting uncomfortably and chewing on her lower lip.

"It's not like that, it's..."

"Whatever," Danny interrupted. "You at least gonna show me out?" he asked.

Susan stood, offering a cordial smile.

"Of course, and it really was nice seeing you," she assured, moving ahead into the entrance hall.

"Yep," Danny muttered, following her out of the room, reaching through the opening and placing a hand on the cold metal of the wrench he'd brought along for this very moment. Susan was still talking ahead of him, but the room had become silent as he tuned out all sound and saw only one image ahead of him. With the adrenaline rising to fever pitch within his body he brought the wrench crashing down onto the back of her skull, a wild glaze over his eyes and a maniacal grin growing as he continued to beat down on the prone body in front of him. Pausing to control the sensation, he went back to the bag and removed the only knife he had been able to find at home. He studied the jagged blade of the bread knife and cursed his rushing to fill the rucksack without interruption. Returning to the body and thrusting the knife down from a height to continuously puncture the torso, sweating profusely and wiping at his brow with his sleeve, he cursed in tongue, a mix of anger, hatred and spittle as the body resisted his attack. Rising from the body in a reddened rage, he kicked out, feeling the unresponsive body offering no defence. A calm came over him, standing tall over his latest conquest.

"No copy needed here. This was a Danny Jemson original," he whispered.

Danny took the instruments and placed them back in the bag before heading to the bathroom to check that he was clear of all markings. He tutted and shook his head as he noticed an area of blood spatter formed on his top. Zipping up his coat to his neck, he resolved that it would need to be burnt when the opportunity arose. However, he had one more task before he could think of heading home. Walking serenely back to the lounge he picked up the phone and dialled as before and steadied his voice.

"Me again," he said coldly. "You might want to send a coroner."

Ben stood solemnly at the window of the address on the sheet of paper, grateful for the darkness hiding him from view, although the hedges surrounding the property would make him virtually invisible to any passer-by on even the clearest summer afternoon. He shook uncontrollably, staring through at the man in the chair watching the box television ahead of him, laughing out loud at the antics on the screen. It was a Christmas episode of *Only Fools and Horses* Ben remembered watching at home with his mum. The man was well into his seventies, his buoyant expression broken intermittently by a severe cough, never truly letting him settle comfortably. He didn't look like he was capable of what Ben had been told. But then did people ever look like they could perform acts others would find intolerable? If that were the case then they wouldn't be such a danger, just a matter of rounding up all those that had *the look*. Ben took a deep breath, thinking of his mother defending herself against his stepfather for the umpteenth time as she called out for him to run to his room and lock the door. It had to stop.

"You can do this," he mumbled.

Ben looked around, ensuring he was alone. He had been assured that the front door would be open until the old man retired for the evening. Just a case of letting himself in and doing what he had been asked, exactly as he had been asked, otherwise he would be stuck with his own problems. Ben placed his hand in his pocket and slowly pulled out the nylon tights he had bought earlier on. He closed his eyes and took a deep breath, taking his first step toward the front door, inadvertently stepping on a loose paving slab, sending him crashing into the windowpane in front of him as he tumbled off balance. As his head thumped against the glass pane, the thud reverberated around the front room, causing the startled old man to spin up from his chair with the speed of someone half his age, alerted by shock and fear. Ben's eyes briefly met with the old man's as he sat in a heap outside the window, unable to move or avert his eyes. The old man's shock turned to anger, as he made his way to meet the adolescent disrupting his evening, shouting about the youth of today. His voice gaining vigour, his temper audible through the bricks and mortar provided Ben with enough initiative to scramble to his feet and find the energy to jump across the pathway and over the front gate. His lungs burned as he strode out down the street he had walked so tentatively in the opposite direction to earlier, arms pumping to evict him from sight while hugging the hedgerows of the surrounding gardens for any kind of cover available. Ben ran until he was back within the confines of the Seven Sisters underground station. Leaning his back against the pillars before the ticket machines, he fell to a squat, rested his head on the cold concrete behind him and let the tears start to rain down once more.

The radio crackled to life as they were heading back from another crank call. They were an all too familiar prank of late. A fabricated accident would see the emergency services screaming to a halt at the reported scene to find a teenager sprawled out, covered in ketchup or whatever the blood of choice was that week, joined by their mates, mobile phones filming the whole thing, as the paramedics went to aid the apparent victim. It was all about the views now. And the hope that one of their videos may just go viral and make them an internet sensation. Sadly it was the type of virus that the emergency services were ill-equipped to prevent.

"Fucking teenagers," Mike barked. "I'd love to be able to get hold of one of them when they're all alone. They'd want us there in a hurry if I ever got that chance," he ranted.

"Never going to happen, Mike. Kids need something to fill their evenings, and for now it's us. It'll pass, always does. Give it a month or two and they'll find some other poor souls to harass," Tom surmised.

"*Anyone in the Green Lanes area? Possible domestic, single casualty.*"

Mike reached down to the handset, acknowledging the call and sending the ambulance into life with sirens wailing and colours blinding as he watched the traffic ahead part to give them the freedom of the road.

"Maybe even a legitimate call," Tom quipped as he strapped himself in with the additional buckle as the speed picked up.

Danny exited the apartment's front entrance, walking purposefully, head raised, surveying the activity around him. He had not encountered a single individual on the descent from Susan's place. All was quiet on the street before him too. He had considered taking a taxi or train home but the thrill was still coursing through him, leaving him oblivious to the chilling winds taking a grip of the city and putting every tree bough to the test. He had done his research and knew the average response time of the emergency services was still over six minutes. He'd be well on his way home by then, just another hardened city resident braving the weather. Striding out into the night he made his way across the quiet streets, leaving the apartment block some four hundred yards behind him when a nagging sound entered his subconscious through the whistling of the wind. Stopping on the empty pathway he looked around to see nothing but the effects the weather was enforcing on the surrounding foliage. Shrugging his shoulders he turned to head back in the direction of home, just as the lights of the ambulance were coming into view and approaching fast. Temporarily frozen, he looked back over his shoulder at the light emitting from the lounge of Susan's apartment where he had been less than two minutes ago. A sinister smile broke out across his face. Turning back in the direction of the ambulance he marched onward.

Too late, I'm afraid.

The ambulance flew over the brow with the navigational system confirming that they were less than thirty seconds out from the destination.

In two hundred and fifty yards, turn right.

Mike was lost in concentration, he was always quiet once the call came through, fully aware that each and every second could make all the difference. Tom took in the surrounding environment, mind drifting to what was going on elsewhere that evening. Another battering for the city at the hands of Mother Nature, he thought as he surveyed the empty streets, empty bar the poor soul fighting the elements on his own. *Hope it's worth it, buddy.* As the ambulance sped onward towards the apartment block ahead, time seemed to stop as Tom's eyes amplified and jaw dropped as he met the gaze of the unknown pedestrian, a sneer etched on the young man's face. Except it wasn't a stranger to Tom, and he couldn't believe who he was looking at.

CHAPTER SEVENTEEN

"Seems busy," Ethan said, resting on the open door of Abbey's Fiat, waiting for her to gather her belongings from the back seat.

"You're surprised?" Abbey asked, fumbling around as her warrant card dropped under the passenger seat. "Crime doesn't take holidays," she said, popping up with a broad smile on her face. "If you want nine to five, Doc, you're in the wrong place."

As they made their way across the car park, the activity only intensified and by the time they were fifty yards from the main entrance it was clear this was anything but normal. The pride of the Fleet Street press were blocking access to the doors while two ageing officers did their best to repel the constant tide of bodies moving back and forth, hollering questions to which no answer was readily expected. Fighting his way through in the opposite direction, Kevin Johnson used his solid frame to knock a couple of the keener journalists from their front-row placing, trying to suppress an all-out grin as he pretended to ignore the glares of frustration and maltreatment directed at him. Abbey and Ethan both smiled amiably as Johnson raised his eyebrows at the situation behind him.

"What can you do?" he asked openly.

"How about not leave cryptic clues before disappearing off home," Abbey countered.

Johnson's smile lessened as he searched for an answer.

"And what's all this about?" Ethan asked, nodding back at the masses, saving Johnson from further examination.

"That makes my minor indiscretion pretty much redundant," he said, directly to Abbey.

"How so?" she asked.

"Because, behind door number five, waiting for your very arrival is a guy claiming to be our copycat."

"Bollocks!" Abbey snapped loudly, drawing attention from a couple of reporters keen to scoop any titbits of information to push their story toward the top of their editor's pile.

"While I may not put it quite so eloquently, my sentiment has to be the same," Ethan said in a far more reserved tone.

PC Johnson tilted his head, and shrugged his shoulders. "All I know, Meadows is waiting for you two before proceeding. Maybe he's the guy, maybe he isn't. He certainly wants us to think he is."

Abbey let out an exasperated sigh, walking at pace toward the gathering, a determined look enough to create the corridor of bodies required to walk into the station unhindered.

"Every case," Ethan commented, walking stride for stride alongside.

"Tell me about it," Abbey replied, pulling at the door handle in anger.

"I know what you're thinking," Meadows said, striding out just to keep pace with them.

"He didn't do it," Abbey and Ethan said in unison.

"I'm sure you're right. But if this is our gift horse..."

Meadows said, raising his hands as they slowed, approaching the door dividing themselves from their waiting confessor.

"Don't look him in the mouth," Ethan said resignedly.

As the door to interview room five creaked open, the sole occupant lifted his head out of his hands and nodded acknowledgement to the two new arrivals. Abbey leant against the wall, looking around, disinterested. Ethan moved forward to the chair opposite their latest distraction. The man was in his late forties, though could easily pass for someone approaching sixty. He had the worn-down look of somebody in the twelfth round of a fight he had no right to be in in the first place. Only his struggle hadn't been in the ring, from the look and smell of him, it had been a gruelling battle against the drink.

"Do you mind?" Ethan asked, pulling the chair from the table.

"No bother, your house," he said.

"My name's Ethan Marshall," Ethan stated, taking his seat. "This is..."

"Pretty," the man interjected.

"So glad you approve," Abbey remarked snidely, holding her position. "And who might you be?"

"I'm the one you've been looking for, darling. You can ride me all the way to a promotion. You can ride me anywhere," he responded.

"Sweet!" Abbey said, pushing herself off the wall so she could approach the table. "You're just a sad, lonely, and desperate for attention little man. If it's not you sitting in that chair, give it a couple of days, and there'll be a queue of fifty more nutjobs just begging to be where you are right now. Gotta get your fifteen minutes. May even be enough to get you a fresh six-pack. I'm guessing you're a special brew kinda guy?"

"You wanna put a muzzle on that one," the man replied evenly, frustratedly trying to rock back on a chair that was bolted to the floor.

Abbey slammed her hands against the table, startling the man, causing him to lose balance and send him falling to the floor.

"Looks like you've had too many already," Abbey said with a smile, watching the man scrambling to his feet with all the grace of a drunk on the high wire, his face flushed, a mixture of anger, embarrassment and exhaustion.

Ethan turned to Abbey sharply. "Out!" he snapped.

"What?" Abbey said, putting her hands up in submission.

"Now," Ethan ordered.

Abbey turned sharply with a huff, slamming the door on her way out. The man was still regaining his bearings, trying to look comfortable as he retook his seat.

"My apologies," Ethan said calmly. "Can we get you a drink or something to eat?"

With his face returning to something like a normal colour, he shook his head disconsolately, not lifting his head from the table.

"While I can't condone her methods, she does have a point," Ethan continued, drawing the man's attention away from the ordinary piece of furniture that had so far fascinated him so.

"Who does?" he asked.

"DI Swift. The young woman who was just..." Ethan began looking over at the door, receiving only a confused look in reply. "Doesn't matter," he continued. "Like I say, her interview technique needs a little work."

"No shit," the man interrupted.

"But, she knows when people are wasting her time, our time, and to be honest, their own time. Do you know what I mean?" Ethan concluded.

The man leant forward in his seat, searching for the right words to put his case across.

"Now I don't know if you're after a bed and a bite to eat, some attention, or even if on some level you truly believe you did these things. What I do know is you're not capable of them. Maybe you even want to be. But you're not. Not physically anyway," Ethan said, before the man could utter a word.

The man went to speak once more, but Ethan raised a hand and continued.

"Clearly you're a man who likes a drink. I'm not judging, everyone has their vice. But you see your right hand?" Ethan said, directing the man's focus. "That shaking. It's permanent, isn't it? A symptom of a need untreated."

The man pulled his sleeves down over both hands, looking anywhere but at Ethan.

"That's one reason. Your reaction to falling, while understandable, there's the second reason. You've got a temper that can go at any time, flare up out of nowhere. You probably feel it's more of a defence mechanism than anything else. Given your current situation, whether through choice or circumstance, I'd imagine you're watching your back before someone even has the chance to place a helping hand upon it? And finally, it took you minutes to recover from a fall of less than two foot. Giving you the benefit that shock would have played some factor in that, it still doesn't show you in the fittest of health. The man we need to speak to is methodical, steady and physically strong. Are you sure you want to carry on down this path? Or are we happy to draw a line under this, get you a bite to eat and a hot drink, and then see you on your way?"

The man's hunched shoulders fell a little further as he offered a sombre nod.

Leaving the old man to ponder over another night of fighting against the cold while feeding his evermore dependant habit, Ethan made his way to the front desk, where DI Swift was apparently coming to the end of a scolding from Superintendant Meadows.

"No excuses, Swift. We treat every lead as a live one until proven otherwise. It isn't dead until it's dead. Are we clear?"

"It was dead. We knew it before we even spoke to him. Any case of any interest, out they come," Abbey argued.

"Are we clear?" Meadows asked again.

"Second one today," the desk sergeant interjected, drawing a glare from Tony Meadows. "Had a young lad in here earlier today mumbling about responsibility," he continued, oblivious to Meadows' ever-furrowing brow.

"You see?" Abbey exclaimed, lifting an arm toward her newly found supporter.

"And what did you tell him?" Meadows asked through gritted teeth.

"Said he should think about what he's doing. And if he really needs to speak with someone, we'll still be here when he comes to that decision," the desk sergeant reasoned.

"So, two claimants, both full of crap, and I now get to go and address the pack of vultures out front, desperate for scraps. Perfect," Meadows lamented, marching off and shaking his head.

"And thank you very much," Abbey said, turning her attention to Ethan.

"What, you thought you handled that well then did you? You let him dictate the situation, Abbey. We already had one hindrance to this case in the room, I didn't need two," Ethan reasoned.

"Your case now is it?" Abbey asked pointedly, walking away.

"Abbey," Ethan called after her.

"Whatever, Doc, let me know when you've cracked it."

Superintendent Meadows held his ground, following the trail of an aeroplane taking holidaymakers away to sunnier, calmer climes, whilst waiting for the melee to subside. Reporters continued to jostle for position as questions rained in from all angles, making each one less comprehensible than the one preceding it. As the plane decreased in stature, making its way ever closer to its destination, Meadows returned his attention to the throng before him, a deep sigh and a low forced cough enough to hush the pack.

"I realise there will be questions, and many of them, from yourselves, and from the constituents of the London area," Meadows began. "Let me start by clarifying the situation we are currently at, as opposed to the conjecture and information obtained from the grapevine that you are so happy to feed from. As has been reported, there have been two crime scenes that would appear to lay reverence to infamous crimes of the past."

"We're told the first was a Manson copy. Who was the other? Do you expect more?" a reporter petitioned rapid-fire, from the middle of the huddle.

"The first we believe was a purely staged event, with the victim having already died of natural causes, some days earlier. And while we will not go into detail, the second victim can be confirmed as Lisa Cole. Her parents have been informed and they are willing to assist us in any way they can." Meadows continued as if not hearing the questions. "This is now an ongoing investigation, and should we have more information, well, I'm sure you'll know before we do," Meadows concluded, moving to re-enter the station.

"Can you confirm she was a working girl?"
"What does the victimless murder mean?"
"Any truth in having a confessor already?"
"Ethan Marshall back on the force, Tony? Is he up to it?"

The questions came in a barrage, the last two as clear as

glass, cutting through the hubbub of the surrounding mass and grabbing Meadows' attention, turning to readdress the gathering.

"The speed of your information never fails to disappoint me," he said dryly, "and, as with any investigation of this profile, we unfortunately attract those that may be looking to promote their own self-interests ahead of ably assisting us in a positive resolution. And, I have no doubt, if we won't give them the time they desire, some of you will be only too happy to do so."

"We've been here before haven't we, Superintendent?" a reporter called out, pushing himself to the front of the pack.

It had been eight years ago when Ron Mayhew had walked into the very station behind him and claimed that he was responsible for the killing of two university students, and if he wasn't detained immediately, he wouldn't be held accountable for his future actions. At the time he had been treated as another fame-hungry aspirant who was politely turned away with the forewarning that wasting police time was a punishable crime, and that it was in his interests not to attract such attention onto himself. Superintendent Meadows had been Detective Chief Inspector at the time, and though he had implored for his own superintendent to take heed of Mr Mayhew, he had been overruled and told not to waste his own time on such characters of self-delusion. It wasn't until another six students had suffered at the hands of the man who couldn't control his actions that Ron Mayhew was brought to justice. The superintendent was laid out to pasture under the guise of retirement, allowing DCI Tony Meadows to become Superintendent Meadows, but he had never shaken the tag of being associated with one of London's lowest points in criminal justice.

"Sadly, far too often I think we can agree," Meadows retorted. "Crimes of this nature are all too prevalent in our city, our country and around the world. Each and every piece of information we receive will be investigated to the fullest."

"And Ethan Marshall?" another reporter repeated.

"Ethan Marshall," Meadows replied, grateful for the change of direction. "Ethan Marshall is an extremely talented individual who is offering counsel on an ongoing foundation. If he were not up to it, as you put it, I am sure he would not have volunteered his services to aid us once more. Ladies and gentlemen, I think we are done here," he concluded, taking his leave into the sanctity of the station as a torrent of voices amalgamated into a single furore once more.

CHAPTER EIGHTEEN

"You gonna stare at that coffee all night?" Mike asked.

The shift had finished over ninety minutes ago, and Tom had sat in the canteen area stirring his black coffee relentlessly, lost in the mini-whirlpool he had created while Mike continued to speak at him. It had been another long evening, spanning the length and breadth of the city, five call-outs and another fatal casualty. A young man in his mid-twenties had run his car through the barrier of an elevated roundabout and plummeted to the asphalt below, managing to pin his upper body to the driver's seat with three of the railings on his way down. A night of activity would usually bring the best out of him, but Tom had hardly spoken a word to his partner all night.

"Are you going to just keep talking all night?" Tom replied.

"There he is. Welcome back to the land of the living. What is the matter with you? You're normally well pumped up on a night like tonight."

"Just got stuff on my mind. Your concern's touching, but really, it's not necessary," Tom said with a wry smile.

"Is this still about the girl in the apartment? Jesus, Tom, she makes it or she doesn't. Time and fate will make that decision. That's the nature of the beast, you know that. You've got to be able to let them go. Can you imagine how it'd be if we carried around the weight of every call-out that doesn't end well? You need to get out, meet people. This job can't be your only thing, Tom, it'll consume you. Christ, get a hobby, make friends, come out for a drink every once in a while."

"I have friends," Tom said dryly.

"Who?"

"You for a start."

Mike let out a sigh, shaking his head. "Work colleagues maybe."

"I have friends," Tom continued sullenly. "In fact, I've got a friend doing a favour for me tonight."

"Great, then you're free to come out and have a drink this evening," Mike posed.

"I am indeed," Tom replied, lifting Mike's spirits. "But I won't be."

"One drink, Tom, a little something to relieve the tension."

"Maybe another time," Tom said, lifting himself from his chair and donning his jacket. "Here comes your coven of nurses now," Tom continued, winking at his partner and hastily making his exit down the corridor to the main entrance of the hospital, tipping his cap and saying his goodnights to the orderlies on his way out.

"Take it he's not meeting us there?" one of the nurses asked, taking the seat Tom had vacated.

"Another time," Mike said with a smile, taking the hand of the senior nurse of the group, who squeezed it back, bending down and kissing the top of his head.

"Still not sure why you bother to make the effort, Michael," she said.

"Because one time he'll say yes," he said, pausing with a smirk. "Plus you witches scare the life out of him! He's harmless."

CHAPTER NINETEEN

Abbey walked through the front door, ensuring she held a scowl in place as she surveyed the hallway. Keys hanging on the rack, shoes neatly placed on the mat and coat hanging over the stairway banister, everything as it should be. Tutting loudly, she dropped her bag and coat on the doormat in a heap and strode off, the scowl transforming into a curious frown as a mix of sound and smells travelled to meet her from the kitchen.

"What the hell is this?" Abbey said bluntly, stopping Ethan mid-chorus, just as he was reaching for an unattainable note.

"The food or the music?" Ethan asked cheerily. "Cos this is steak," he continued, shuffling the pan over the hob, "peppercorn sauce on the way. Fresh salad in the fridge, and skinny fries in the oven."

"I like chunky chips," Abbey said.

"Of course you do. And if I'd have done chunky chips, you'd prefer skinny fries."

Abbey suppressed a smile and walked around the kitchen, appraising the activities.

"And this crap?" she asked, pointing to the stereo.

"Well, this is a little treat for you. I said I'd get you a CD."

"Thunder?"

"It is," Ethan confirmed.

"I don't like it."

"That's just because you're mad with me. Maybe best to have a listen later on, or when I'm not here."

"And why would I be mad at you?"

"Well..." Ethan began.

"And you think this makes it better?" Abbey persevered.

"Hoped more than thought," Ethan said earnestly, cutting into the steaks and watching the faintest trail of blood seep into the pan.

"So, sit down, shut up, and accept my attempt at an apology," he continued.

Abbey narrowed her eyes and pursed her lips as she made her way over to the table that had already been laid out in anticipation of her arrival.

Having served Abbey and poured her a glass of red wine, Ethan took his seat and raised his glass of Diet Coke which Abbey clinked begrudgingly.

"It's good," she said, slicing into the tender steak. "No wine for you? There's beers in the fridge."

"I don't do wine, they all taste the same to me, or beer for that matter, same applies."

"All taste the same?" Abbey replied in disgust. "There are people that dedicate their lives to wine. Sacrilege... Lucy would have you strung up if she could hear you now!"

"I am sorry, Abbey."

"Forget about it. It's only wine, I won't tell her."

"Not about the wine..."

"I said forget about it, Doc," Abbey said, cutting across him. "Best not to dwell over things that can only sour whilst simmering. Plus, there's a small part of me that thinks I could have probably handled the situation a little better," she said with a grin.

"Best not to dwell..."

"My grandmother had a saying for every occasion. And while the majority don't make any sense, I can remember every single one of them," Abbey said.

"I like it. Sounds like a wise woman," Ethan stated as a silence fell over the table, both enjoying the meal and in Abbey's case, the wine.

"You sing terribly by the way," Abbey said, breaking the silence as she was coming to the end of the meal and picking at the remaining lettuce leaves with her fingers. "I mean really, really bad," she said with a giggle.

"You just didn't appreciate it because you were angry," Ethan countered. "I'll have you know my mother always said I had a beautiful singing voice!"

As Ethan cleared the table and ensured that the kitchen was back to the fine state he had originally found it in, Abbey poured another glass of wine, draining the last remnants of the bottle until convinced that none were to be wasted.

"Best case, worst case," she said as Ethan retook his seat and started on his own refill.

"Probably one and the same," Ethan replied.

"Outside of that one then."

"In whose eyes?" Ethan asked.

"Just yours."

"Best case," he mumbled, rubbing a hand across his mouth. "An early one then. Probably only my second involvement with the Met. A young girl, I think she was eight or nine years old, had gone missing. A real case of up and vanished, no leads, no trace, just gone. Happy at home, doing well in school for her age, no reason to run and no sign of being taken."

"So what was your break?" Abbey asked.

"Well, the parents were understandably inconsolable. But that meant they were of little to no help in building up an image or profile that could be worked from. That left the neighbours and surrounding community," he said. "Shame that it takes children being harmed or crimes being committed to bring the best out of society. Anyway, everyone obviously wanted to do all they could and put themselves out for searches and trying to remember scraps of information that were maybe irrelevant before whatever happened, happened. And there was one guy, the uncle as it turned out. Who, as crazy as it sounds when you say it aloud, cared just a little too much, wanted to help too much."

"And it was him?" Abbey inferred.

"Found the girl in the boot of his car, gagged and bound with a straw from a water bottle pierced through the tape covering her mouth. His cases packed and on the back seat. Other than being half-starved and scared to death, no physical harm had come to her."

"Lucky girl. And the worst case?"

"Each and every one we don't get to before it's too late," Ethan replied, taking a long swallow of his Coke. "You?"

Abbey laughed softly.

"Bag snatcher in Whitehall," she said. "Could've been Jack the Ripper to me. That was my first ever arrest. And I knew I wanted to be a copper. Not as exciting as yours I'm afraid."

"The less that are, the better it is," Ethan said. "Worst?"

"Honestly?" Abbey asked. "I'd have to say the one we're on now. It's the biggest case I've ever been given, and it feels like we're running into one brick wall, only to turn in a different direction and hit another."

"It might be slow, but progress is being made. We know more than we did before, and probably not as much yet as we will tomorrow," Ethan said, finishing off the remnants of a drink that had already been drained.

"Shake enough trees and eventually you'll get a coconut," Abbey mused with a smile.

"Grandma?"

Abbey nodded, savouring the last few drops of her wine.

"Right then, bed," Ethan said, getting to his feet.

"My, my, the apology continues," Abbey said with a devilish grin, causing Ethan to blush.

CHAPTER TWENTY

While others throughout the city had been enjoying their evening meal, a young man had been tending to a cuisine of his own personal creation, ensuring the proverbial watched pot had boiled nicely.

Reed Morgan walked down Shaftesbury Avenue, hands deep in the pockets of his leather trench coat, squinting through his matted hair as he leaned into the unforgiving wind that continued to assault the city, checking every recess currently playing host to the desperate and the destitute. *Bet they're regretting their lifestyle choice now,* he thought, as he watched London's great ignored civilisation trying to fit their worldly goods in door fronts and alleyways while hauling each blanket and sleeping bag around them a little tighter for anything resembling warmth. Reed continued to survey the scene before him, locking into a stare with an elderly transient feverishly trying to find a vein, becoming more agitated each time the plunger was drawn back to no bodily reaction.

"Fuck you looking at?" the man asked hoarsely.

"Just thinking that I couldn't imagine a better way for you to spend your hard-earned money than on that shit. I mean, you look like you're well fed, watered, and no doubt you've got a nice place in the suburbs. What more could you ask for?" Reed replied mockingly, holding the man's gaze.

"Fuck off," the man said, turning his back on the unknown visitor, continuing to try and find blood among the numerous established track marks.

"Try between your fingers," Reed said with a sneer, shaking his head and continuing along the road.

Stop it, this is too easy.

Towards the end of an alleyway, a figure sat alone on a crate, pushed up against the building wall, arms wrapped tightly around his torso and knees drawn up to the same position, shivering uncontrollably, no blankets or coat for protection. Turning back to view where he'd just walked, Reed could see that every crevice had been occupied and without venturing on to pastures new, there was no further shelter to be found for the incumbent selection. With his choice made, Reed took his hands from his pockets and strode purposefully onward, forming various welcoming expressions as he did so, closing in on his target.

"Hey man, no way you can stay out here all night. This weather'll be the death of you," Reed said, cupping his hands to his mouth and blowing, "and me."

The figure had been younger than Reed had expected, maybe just a year or two older than himself. He looked gaunt and withered, more bone than muscle. His eyes sat deep, and looked darkened through lack of sleep, or fear, or maybe lack of sleep due to fear. He rocked back and forth, looking intensely into Reed's stare, deciding whether he could be trusted.

"Who're you?" the young man asked, his body in constant motion.

"Rick," Reed replied, "from the outreach centre."

"That centre's closed," he said, shaking his head, withdrawing into the wall behind him, unblinking.

"Building might be, but the outreach doesn't ever really close. Not when we're still needed. And on nights like this, this is when we're needed most. Can't tell me you want to be out in this," Reed continued, looking around at the strain the winds placed on their surroundings. "What's your name?" Reed asked.

The young man held his stare, shuffling back on the crate, then turned away to look back up the street, searching for a vacant aperture.

"Fine, I'm not looking for a fight," Reed said, exasperated. "If you make it till morning, drop by the centre. Just thought the idea of a hot meal, and maybe even a bed for a night may be of some comfort," Reed finished, turning away to leave.

"Stewart," the young man said meekly.

Reed grinned, holding his ground, looking out across the gathering cloudline darkening menacingly as the night fought off the last of the daylight, before returning to Stewart with a comforting nod.

"Well then, Stewart, let's get you something to eat," he offered, waving the young man off the crate.

Entering the flat Stewart was decidedly more relaxed in his new acquaintance's presence, striding off ahead of his virtuous keeper and checking out each room like a prospective tenant.

"Nice place," Stewart called from one of the two bedrooms. "How long you say you've been trying to sell it for?"

"Around two months," Reed replied in a hushed tone, trying to keep any anger from his voice as he closed the front door, checking for any disturbance from the adjacent floors.

"No, I like it," Stewart continued, appearing from the bathroom. "Homely."

"Very kind of you to say so, Stewart. Why don't you take a seat in the kitchen? I'll get a bath run for you, and once you've eaten you can get cleaned up. Sound good?"

"Can't believe you do this on your own time, Rick. Not sure where I'd be without the city shelters, but this is something else. This is above and beyond."

Reed walked back into the kitchen with a kindly smile, the water running hard in the background, drumming against the bare bathtub before softening slightly as the water level increased.

"We all have our calling," he said, moving over to the fridge. "Omelette? I'm afraid I'm not much of a cook."

"Lovely. I thought you meant a café or something when you offered food. I mean, I know the shelter guys like to give you food and drink rather than money. Because, obviously they know the money goes on other things. Some buy drink, but not the drink they have in mind if you know what I mean," Stewart rambled as Reed cracked eggs into a bowl and whisked proficiently before dropping them into a pan warming on the hob.

"I always found water goes well with every meal," Reed answered, passing a glass from the draining board to Stewart while he transferred the tossed omelette onto a plate, and placed it on the table as Stewart returned to his seat.

"Tuck in. I'll go and check the water," Reed said, taking his leave from the room.

Reed returned to the kitchen area as Stewart was scraping the last morsels of food onto his fork and rubbing his fingers across the plate's surface to spare nothing. Striding with purpose across the short spacing between them, Reed's calm and friendly demeanour was no more, a focused and resolute look etched across his face as he lifted the necktie in his right hand, grabbing the far end of the material in his free fist, thrusting it over Stewart's head and wrenching it back sharply into his oesophagus before he had even had time to react to the sound of the feet approaching at pace. Gasping for breath as the wind left his body, Stewart clawed at the tie restricting his air supply. Reed hauled the tie tighter and twisted the material in his grasp, feeling the strain against the flesh of the neck as the chair wavered and toppled away, leaving Stewart fighting with his upper body while his legs flayed frantically, searching for solid ground. Reed continued to lift up and inward, never allowing the weakened body of his guest to feel the comfort of support from which to fight from. With the battering his body had taken from his recent way of life, the will could only last so long as Stewart moved briefly in and out of consciousness until all fight was gone, leaving only a motionless body adjoined to a steadily breathing Reed by the strained strands of a tie.

Reed Morgan prodded at the rotating mass within the pot with a wooden spoon, forcing it to revolve vertically and reveal Stewart's desiccated features. He had been surprised by just how easy the process had been, aside from the difficulty of trying to undress the dead weight. With so little muscle and having suffered from weeks of malnutrition, the neck had provided little to no resistance when being separated from its owner. Taking a cursory sweep of the apartment, Reed turned the hob gas off, watching the remaining heat within the water simmer and subside before making his exit from the apartment in the same quiet fashion in which he had arrived, taking a business card from his jeans back pocket and making his way to the call phone a little over half a mile away.

CHAPTER TWENTY-ONE

Tony Meadows was already in mid-conversation with two men leaning against their combo-van, adorned with the company logo, *Pipe Dreams* when Abbey and Ethan arrived at the base of the low-rise flats.

"Looks like our perp has a taste for the finer things now," Abbey said as they approached the superintendent.

"In property, maybe," Ethan countered, looking around at the pleasantly gardened surroundings, evaluating the growing crowd forming on the spectator side of the police tape.

"Human nature to return to review your work," Ethan continued, checking faces. "Have anyone that worked the other crime scenes assess our macabre gathering. Anyone they think they recognise, we look at for questioning. We need to start making things happen," he concluded, acknowledging Meadows with a subtle nod.

"Sir," Abbey offered.

"This is Bob," Meadows introduced, pointing to the larger, older man. "And this is his apprentice and son, Darren. Picked up a message on their machine this morning. Call-out required, door would be open for them, blockage to the drains."

"Lad shouldn't have to see a thing like that," Bob interrupted.

"Suffice to say, there's no blockage," Meadows concluded.

"Nice," Abbey said, pointing to the company name on the van.

"Thanks," Bob said. "That was his fault too," he continued, looking at Darren. "Always been a dreamer. Until he decided he wanted to work with his old man. And look what that brings him."

"Ready for the tour?" Meadows asked.

"Lead on," Ethan said as they made their way over the lawn and into the entrance hall of the block. "How about a little forewarning on the way this time though."

"No ID as yet," Meadows said, climbing the stairs, breathing heavily, "though clearly wasn't in a well way even before all this, judging by the state of the body. That's in the bath by the way. Gonna need dental records to put a face to the head. That's on the stove."

"What?" Abbey cut in.

"Oh yeah, he went to town on this one. And we found his hands and feet..."

"In bin bags in the wardrobes," Ethan said softly alongside the superintendent's same wording. Meadows smiling resignedly, impressed.

"Doc, you need to lighten up on your reading material. What happened to you and your love of Harry Potter, hell, even throw some Lee Child in if you need some excitement. None of these appealing to you?"

"Was he fed?" Ethan asked.

Meadows nodded solemnly, pushing the front door of the apartment open for them to step inside.

"Broken eggshells and milk left on the side, plate on the

table in the kitchen. Although we won't know official stomach contents until later on."

"You know who this one is then I presume?" Abbey asked, surveying the flat, looking past and through the busy analysts on the scene.

"Had an idea once a plumbing company was involved," Ethan said.

"So?" Abbey enquired.

"Well, I'd lay a pound to your penny that the deceased was homeless. Entered the premises of his own free will under the pretence of a hot meal and maybe somewhere to stay."

"And you know this because who did what to whom?" Abbey pried.

"Dennis Nilsen did strangulations, drowning, dismemberment and boiling to numerous victims, the majority of who were homeless or male street workers," Ethan explained as Abbey walked into the bathroom, studying the back of the cadaver missing its hands, feet and head. Blood had discoloured the water, but the grey, skeletal features of the body's mass were still visible, although no physical markings were noticeable to the remaining torso.

"He was known as the kindly killer," Ethan continued, as Abbey rejoined them in the kitchen, shaking her head.

"Just look at all the kindness in this room," she said, looking into the pot on the stove, wincing. "What the Samaritans wouldn't do to have this guy on their payroll. And of course we've got nothing?" she asked Meadows.

"Another property that's on the market, countless fingerprints of course."

"Fuck's sake," Abbey muttered dejectedly.

"One clear print on an eggshell," Meadows said with a grin.

Abbey lifted her head, beaming, grabbing her superior officer and planting a kiss on his forehead.

"Yes!" she exclaimed, "you said he'd make a mistake," she continued, looking at Ethan.

"Get off me," Meadows chortled, pushing Abbey away.

"Let's be sure before we get too excited," Ethan added.

"The eggshell, Doc. Who else is it going to be? We're gonna get the careless bastard," she replied brightly.

"Sir," a young officer said, poking his head around the doorframe, attracting the attention of everyone within the small kitchen space.

"Sir, there's been another one."

CHAPTER TWENTY-TWO

Superintendent Meadows had been left behind, kerbside, shaking his head and wondering what he was going to tell the chief commissioner, who had been imploring a swift result to ease his own pressures from above, and how much detail he was going to feed to the press to relieve their constant clamour and maybe even draw those forward too afraid to go to the police directly. It was a balancing act he had never enjoyed, and still had some way to mastering.

Ethan and Abbey headed out toward the second scene with relative ease. The morning rush hour traffic had long since subsided and all that was left to contend with was the constant congestion London provided to all its motorists every hour of the working day.

"How far away did they say?" Ethan asked.

"Quarter of an hour's walk, probably twenty-five minutes in the car," she said, tutting.

"Close enough," Ethan said.

"Two in one night? That's some escalation. I got the impression he wasn't an impulse kinda guy."

"I guess we're about to find out," Ethan conceded.

"So what do we know, Joe?" Abbey asked, tapping her hands on the steering wheel as another eighties classic found its way onto Magic FM.

"Fifty points," Ethan said, looking at the radio.

"What?"

"Fifty points. Who's this?" Ethan asked.

"I thought we were talking about the case?"

"Fine. If you don't know, just say so."

Abbey sighed heavily. "Terence Trent D'Arby. So there's my fifty points," she said, stifling a nonchalant grin. "So what do we know?"

"Well, I know that the points on offer need to be much lower, or the questions tougher."

"Ethan!" Abbey said, fighting her laughter.

"All right. We know that the chosen locations are either abandoned or currently empty, like those up for sale."

"Except this one isn't," Abbey added, pointing toward her distant destination.

"Leaving that aside," Ethan replied, "logic would therefore suggest that A, he is involved in property, an estate agent maybe. Which we've ruled out already. B, an opportunist, but more than one site would again suggest not, or C, meticulous in both his research and his actions."

"Which makes two kills in one evening all the more unexpected," Abbey chipped in.

"And all the more dangerous," Ethan supposed, leaving the thought hanging between the two of them as silence fell in the car.

Having watched the brake lights of the same Ford Focus bounce on and off for the last mile or so and listened to more mellow music from the Magic airways as the traffic came to a near stagnant crawl, Abbey glanced all around, tapping her hands impatiently as Ethan continued to look out of the side window at all and nothing at the same time.

"So how did they get caught?" she asked. "The originals I mean. Those that we are seeing the copies of now."

"The copies specifically?" Ethan asked, turning his attention to Abbey. "Or the most infamous serials?"

"Dealer's choice," Abbey offered.

"Okay. Well, Manson was arrested originally for vandalising a national park. It wasn't until one of his followers feared further reprisal that she confessed to the Manson murders. Dennis Nilsen, as you know, got caught because he couldn't dispose of the victims and when trying to do so blocked his drains, attracting the attention of local services."

"Unintentionally though," Abbey quipped.

"Indeed. Ted Bundy, and you can add Jeffrey Dahmer, Albert DeSalvo and John Wayne Gacy to the list. They got caught because of a failed abduction, or in Gacy's case, letting a victim go. Three major cases that were handed eyewitnesses."

"He let him go, by choice? Why would you do that?" Abbey asked.

"Who knows? Remorse, the desire to be caught? Albert DeSalvo, the Boston Strangler..."

"I do know," Abbey interrupted, exasperated.

"Sorry. Did you know it was one of the first high-profile cases to utilise a criminal profiler? He had the Strangler pegged as an escaped patient from the Boston psychiatric hospital, who could show no emotion and held no standing in society. It's said that he had them looking for Mr Hyde, when they were really after Dr Jekyll."

"Not your profession's finest hour then, Doc," Abbey said with a grin, steering off into an opulent housing estate.

"Anyway, he was caught because during an attack on one of his female victims, he caught sight of himself in the mirror and was so disgusted by what he saw that he fled, begging the woman not to go to the police, which of course she did, and when questioned, held his hands up to being the elusive Strangler," Ethan finished as the car came to a stop outside of the latest prospective puzzle piece.

"No crowd of onlookers here," Abbey said, getting out of the car and acknowledging the single officer outside of the front door.

"More of a curtain-twitching environment I'd say."

"So you're telling me that they all got caught because of their own undoing? Nothing to do with good police work?" Abbey asked.

"We wait for the mistake. Policing plays a part, but ultimately, we wait for the mistake," Ethan said as they made their way up to the property.

CHAPTER TWENTY-THREE

He sat on the bench across the street, happily feeding the pigeons breadcrumbs as they flocked around his feet, pecking at the ground for scraps of food, or at each other should one's feeding space be encroached upon. Looking for all the world to see like he didn't have a care in the world, Tom had sat dropping his crumbs from behind his darkened glasses, white cane by his side for almost three hours, his eyes never leaving the number twenty-three front door directly opposite his position. The chill factor still resided although the strength of the wind itself had dropped dramatically as Tom fought the urge to shiver, waiting for movement from within. Just as impatience was building within him, the red door of all his focus cracked partially open as a woman's voice could be heard shouting back into the main frame of the house, although no words were distinguishable as they perished on the breeze. A stout woman in her early fifties rocked out from the porchway pulling a small luggage case behind her as she waddled up the street in the direction of the bus stop, breathing heavily by the time she had reached her fourth step.

A little break away would be handy, probably just thinks she's too young for a shopping trolley, he thought as he watched her wide but diminutive figure ever decreasing in stature. Having blindly fed the winged rats for another five minutes, Tom waited until no activity was visible and made his way steadily across the street to number twenty-three.

Danny sat at his computer console taking on the good and the bad of the World of Warcraft, choosing to ignore the light rap emanating from the front hallway. Having dedicated as much time as he had to his latest quest, it was no surprise with the ease with which he was now progressing, and he wasn't going to put his mission on hold for some door-to-door salesman peddling his wares, or worse, religion. The knocking grew louder which Danny was content to ignore and play absent until it became a constant repetition preventing him from concentrating on the matter in hand.

"Just fuck off," he grumbled as he stood to his feet and made his way downstairs. "What?" he asked, pulling the door open sharply and addressing the man before him. "Not buying it, not praying to it," he said coarsely.

"Well, I'm not selling it, or preaching it," Tom replied evenly.

"Who are you then?" Danny asked.

"Just a friend... of your mother's."

"She's out, never mind. See ya. I'll tell her you dropped by," Danny said, closing the door until meeting the resistance of Tom's hand, holding steady against the pressure, placing a boot next to the frame of the door.

"How about I wait inside?" he said with steely look.

"Could be a while," Danny said casually, pushing for any slack in resistance.

"I'll wait inside," Tom answered, pushing the door a little further back, making his way into the house. "You can close the door now."

Danny stood in the living-room doorway as Tom took a seat on the settee, perusing his surroundings. The room wasn't dirty but had a haphazard feel to it, if it wasn't on the floor, then it wasn't untidy. The only things without obstacle were the television set, and the remote, free of clutter on the arm of the lounger.

"What you looking at?" Danny snapped.

"Do you never give your mother a hand around the house?" Tom asked. "Tidy, wash up, hoover?"

"You live in a palace then do you?"

"Far from it. But it is clean. But then that's me," Tom said, shrugging his shoulders. "I like things clean. No clutter, no mess, no loose ends," he continued.

"What did you say your name was?" Danny asked, his voice shaky.

"I didn't," Tom said, lifting himself to his feet.

"Well, what is it?"

"It's not important."

"And my mum knows you?" Danny asked, finding vigour, drawing himself to his full height.

"She does not," Tom said coolly.

"Well, she'll be back any minute, and if she finds you in our house..." Danny countered.

"She won't," Tom said, shaking his head slowly.

"Well, what the fuck do you want then?" Danny asked, backing away as Tom advanced on him steadily. "Just take what you want."

"I don't want anything," he said, stopping short as Danny

backed into the hallway mirror, glancing from side to side, visibly shaking.

"Then why are you here?" he pleaded.

"Simply to teach."

"Oh God!" Danny said, as tears began to fall down his face.

CHAPTER TWENTY-FOUR

"So do I leave the keys with you?" Abbey asked the attending officer by the front door, looking over at her car with a grin.

"Piss off," he said, "ma'am."

"I guess I have to open the door for myself too?" she cracked, looking at Ethan. "Won't last ten minutes," she persisted, shaking her head at the officer disapprovingly with half a smile.

The door led through a small porch where shoes were stacked on the rack, and coats hung accordingly, directly into the lounge. The lounge itself was well decorated and held a grandeur befitting its large scale and was evidently a place of pride for the homeowner. Wooden cabinets housed decorative antiques and ornaments, while wall hangings filled the edge of the room without appearing untidy. The prized possession and centrepiece was clearly the piano, sitting proudly in the corner, gleaming as if with superiority, key cover lifted and sheet music in place, demanding to be played. A young woman in her mid-twenties was sat ashen-faced on the armchair, wiping at her eyes constantly with her sleeves, trying to control her hyperventilating while a man of similar age perched on the arm next to her stroked her back reassuringly.

"She shouldn't have to be here," the young man shouted across the room as Abbey and Ethan entered. "Why does she need to see all of this?" he said, gesturing to the police activity surrounding them.

One of the officers on scene placed a calming hand on his shoulder, sitting him back onto the arm of the chair, speaking gently until the man conceded defeat and returned to consoling the young woman.

"Been like that since we got here. Wanting to fight all and sundry that get within three feet of him or his girl," the officer said, addressing Abbey and Ethan.

"Who are they?" Ethan asked.

"That's the daughter, Sarah, the one who called it in, and that's her husband, Craig, he came back just after we arrived. Apparently he'd been down the gym and so hadn't known she'd been trying to contact him until he was getting changed afterwards. They're living here with her mother while they save for their own place."

"Father?" Abbey asked.

"Passed away some years ago apparently. Was just the two of them for a while, and then your livewire over there moved in after they were married, little over a year ago."

"You get their statements, where they're going to stay?" Abbey asked.

"Yep, all done, they're staying with her aunt, easy enough to follow up on. Daughter's a mess, being here isn't going to benefit anyone."

Abbey nodded in agreement and went over to the couple, squatting to the level of the daughter.

"Hey, I'm Detective Swift," she introduced softly. "I'm so sorry for your loss. Why don't you get yourself off and we can speak with you later on, should we need to."

"About time," the husband snapped, shaking his head, aiding his wife from the chair.

"Just look after her," Abbey shot back.

"You were at the gym, right?" Ethan asked as the couple stood before him.

"Yeah," he replied, starting to leave.

"Do they supply towels there? It's just at my gym…"

"What? Yes, they supply towels. Not sure why you'd want to share a towel with fifty other men though?"

"So you take your own?" Ethan posed.

"Christ, yes, I take my own. Can we go now?" he said irritably.

"Please," Ethan said, stepping aside.

"Care to share?" Abbey asked as they watched the couple leave, the comforting arm again massaging his wife's back as the shaking of emotional outpouring began.

"He looked good, he wasn't in gym gear."

"So?"

"He showered, he got changed. Only problem with that is he uses his own towel, which means he went to his locker or bag or whatever. Human nature says you'd check your phone. Everyone likes to be liked. Society dictates it," Ethan mused.

"You like the husband," Abbey suggested.

"Not even a little bit," Ethan replied.

"You want to at least check out the bathroom before you make your citizen's arrest, son?" a deep voice said from behind them.

"Hey, Jameson, what you doing here?" Abbey asked, turning and giving him a kiss on the cheek.

Pat Jameson's blushing was visible even through his thick grey beard. Dressed in a three-piece suit and wearing a grey trilby, it would've been hard to distinguish the ageing detective from those he was trying to catch when he first came onto the job.

"Hey, kiddo," he said with a wink, "and Mr Marshall, will wonders never cease?" he continued, proffering his hand.

"Hey, Irish, long time," Ethan said, accepting the handshake. "You not had enough yet then?"

"Nor you it would seem. Thought wild horses couldn't have dragged you back."

"Irish?" Abbey chipped in.

"Jameson, like the whisky," Ethan explained.

"My protégée, or project," Jameson said, smiling. "Taught her all I know and she can't put things like that together."

"That took care of Monday," Abbey replied. "Been fending for myself ever since."

"Lucky you've got such a pretty face to hide that tongue of yours," Jameson reasoned, waving a finger. "You want to head upstairs?" he asked.

"You all right with stairs?" Abbey asked mockingly, as Jameson raised the back of his hand to her and led the way.

"Got your hands full with that one."

"You notice downstairs, and the bedroom too?" Jameson asked, pushing the door open opposite the bathroom to show an empty room, the crime-scene team coming out from the main attraction at his request.

"Spotless," Abbey said, poking her head into the bedroom, "nothing taken."

"Attagirl. Which means?"

"Really? Are we going to do this until you retire?"

Jameson folded his arms and waited.

"Never too old to learn," Ethan added with a smirk.

"Which means it wasn't an attempted robbery, leaving a predetermined act or an accident," she surmised.

Jameson turned and motioned them into the bathroom, much to the frustration of Abbey, shaking her head bemusedly as she entered.

"Early prognosis, Doctor?"

"What do we know?" Ethan asked.

"Put a pair of these on and look for yourself," Jameson said, handing him a box of surgical gloves from the sink sill.

Ethan studied the picture before him as he slid his hands into the gloves, passing the box on to Abbey to do the same. A well-dressed woman in her early fifties lay in the empty bathtub, a pair of sheer tights wrapped loosely round her neck, head resting on the tiles behind, looking as if she were in a deep peaceful sleep. Ethan leant in, lifting the head gently forward with two fingers, revealing a tiny spot of red on the white tiling.

"Blunt force trauma," Jameson said as Ethan looked his way, placing the head back in its restful state. "Long, narrow and pointed," he continued. "There's been a clean-up somewhere. We've got the boys and girls checking every inch of the house."

"Look at the neck, not a mark on it," Abbey stated. "The stocking's an afterthought. They're using the media coverage of our case to try and cover their own."

"They?" Ethan asked.

"He, she, they, whoever. Albert DeSalvo it ain't. This isn't our guy," she proclaimed, rubbing her temples.

"Not unless he's lost all interest," Ethan mumbled. "Looks like this one's all yours, Irish."

"It'll be a pleasure if it's who I think it is," Jameson admitted.

"You like the husband too," Abbey concluded.

"Too much anger in that boy. He's still venting, and doesn't know why it won't pass. I'm sure I can help him," Jameson said with a broad smile.

CHAPTER TWENTY-FIVE

Danny heard the initial crack, and then the spread as the mirror bowed to the pressure as he pushed himself deeper into the wall, going nowhere. His eyes wide with terror, Danny weighed up his escape routes. The door to the kitchen was closed, he'd be caught before he grabbed the handle, and dead ahead, his way was blocked. Tom encroached slowly upon the space between them, looking at the closed door, and then at Danny, disappointment on his face.

"Why so scared? You've already made it quite clear I am unable to do what you are so capable of. And on two occasions no less."

Danny said nothing, looking from the floor to his ever-approaching virtual cohort, now so very real, trembling with every inch of ground conceded.

"Truth is, I need you," Tom offered calmly, "and the bitch probably deserved it."

"She fucking did!" Danny yelled back.

"A team, that's what we are. You and I," Tom continued evenly, "we could do great things together, Danny. Great things. Want to show me your set-up?" Tom asked.

Danny stood, perplexed, weighing up the man before him.

"Come on, I was just playing. If I'd wanted to harm you I'd have done it by now," Tom said with a smile, stepping to the side and gesturing up the stairs so Danny could lead the way.

"I guess," Danny said hesitantly as he relaxed a little, stepping across the doorway and turning up the staircase.

As Danny placed his foot on the first step he saw the arm out of the corner of his eye, flashing forward and back again, generating a vice-like grip around his throat, trapped between forearm and bicep, Tom breathing seamlessly as he pushed his weight into the back of his wayward protégé. Holding fast against the bucking youth, tightening his grasp each time Danny thrashed for forgiveness, choking him to a rest and then easing his grip while he prepared for the next wave of panic-stricken struggle.

"Shhh, it'll all be over soon," Tom whispered as he withdrew the syringe from his jacket pocket, piercing the skin on Danny's neck and pushing the plunger slowly and evenly, the mixture of words and sharp incision providing Danny with enough adrenaline for one final tussle.

Tom held tight against Danny's desperate onslaught, feeling the body go weak and lifting him into a cradle position. Danny's eyes were glazed and searching as his mouth opened intermittently, fish-like, trying to form words that wouldn't make their way into the world.

"What did I give you?" Tom said calmly. "Thirty milligrams of diamorphine. Don't worry, this'll pass, the words will come. We've got a few minutes yet. Why don't you show me that set-up of yours?" he concluded, climbing the staircase as Danny's eyes widened in fear.

"You see this, this isn't good for you," Tom said, waving a finger at the game playing itself out on the computer screen before him.

"It's..." Danny murmured hoarsely, sounding like he hadn't had a drink in days.

"I'm sorry?" Tom replied, spinning the swivel chair to face the prone shell of his captive lying on the bed.

"It's just a game," he husked.

"Such a waste," he said, shaking his head. "A world of information at your fingertips, limitless opportunity. But you'd rather be a fucking goblin."

"What are you going to do to me?" Danny asked, forcing his eyes open as they fought incessantly for rest.

Tom leant forward, resting his elbows on his knees, thumbs underneath his chin as he drummed his fingers together, inches above Danny, watching as his breathing became continually shallow.

"I'm not going to do anything to you," he explained as Danny's eyes closed once more. "But I will wait with you. You see, we're about two minutes in now, which is why you feel so tired, drained. In an attempt to preserve energy, you'll pass into what we'll call a deep sleep. No one likes the term *coma*," he narrated, as Danny lay motionless. "A minute or two in that state, and the shallow breathing will become non-existent, starving the brain of oxygen. As with any form of starvation, the ending is predetermined."

"You let emotion get involved," Danny responded drowsily.

"Hmm," Tom mused, tilting his head. "Interesting final thoughts," he said.

"You said to never do that..." Danny trailed off as he fell into a silent slumber.

Tom stood with a sudden swelling in his chest, his heart

STEVE CORNWELL

beating a little faster as he looked down over the disappointment of misjudged trust making its way from one world to the next.

CHAPTER TWENTY-SIX

"Enjoy your day off?" Mike asked.

"Always do," Tom replied over his shoulder, checking that the vehicle was fully stocked with all the necessary requirements before their shift officially started.

"What, that's it? Not going to fill me in on what you did?"

"Nothing to fill in. Just tying up the loose ends that you never get time to sort."

"This loose end got a name?" Mike asked with a mischievous grin. "One day off and you come back a new man, don't tell me..."

"Bandages," Tom interrupted, jumping down from the back of the ambulance, wiping his hands on a sanitiser cloth. "We need more bandages. And more of these too," he concluded, throwing the cloth at Mike.

"Coffee?" Mike asked, holding his hands up in defeat.

"How's the girl?" Tom countered in a more sombre tone.

"Fighting. She's stabilised, but, she suffered bad, Tom. Chances are if her body pulls through, she'll be in a vegetated state anyway. But hey, who knows, we've seen bigger turnarounds than this, right?" Mike responded, trying to sound positive. "Can only hope they catch the tosser who put her through it."

"They won't," Tom stated, closing the back doors. "Come on, let's get that coffee."

The cafeteria was already in full flow, a mixture of staff coming onto shift grabbing a late breakfast or early lunch and those visiting friends and relatives fighting for the limited seating space with the current hospital residents who were well enough to get around, and use that advantage to arrive before visiting hours were underway. The three elderly ladies serving were all volunteers and had been at the hospital for as long as Mike and Tom could remember, able to read each paying customer and respond accordingly, accurately distinguishing between those that were visiting someone for a sprain, and those whose nearest and dearest were facing a much graver prospect.

"Your fan club's on today then," Tom said, nodding at the three elderly ladies.

"Behave yourself," Mike said under his breath, waving to a table of nurses in the corner, gesturing that they had two spare seats.

"Oh, and your harem's here too, wonderful," Tom taunted as they approached the counter.

"Morning, boys, morning, Mike," the lady with *Maggie* written on her badge greeted them warmly.

"Morning, ladies, how's life treating you?" Mike replied.

"Ladies," Tom acknowledged.

"Coldly. I woke up this morning and look," Eileen said, pressing at her cheeks, "my looks, gone, overnight. Not happy, Thomas," she scoffed.

"It is a crime," Mike offered.

"Two coffees please, one black, one white," Tom said.

"And arthritis is a bitch," Maggie said, already placing the order on a tray.

"We can only hope tomorrow is kinder to us all," Mike quipped, handing over his loose change to pay for the drinks as Tom collected the two cups, leaving the tray on the counter.

"Kinder, some of us just hope there is a tomorrow," the final lady added with a cackle, the attention of the three serving attendants passing to their next patron.

"Old Dorises love a chat don't they?" Tom said, shaking his head and taking a seat within the group of five women.

"Hey, mister," the senior nurse said, addressing Mike and placing a hand on his knee as he sat down. "Still shying away from human interaction then, Tom?" she asked.

"Hardly," Mike said, smirking.

"Really?" the woman said, raising her eyebrows. "Do tell."

"Nothing to tell. Your man's got impure thoughts in his mind and won't let them go. Shouldn't you be doing something about that for him?"

"How do you know I'm not?" she responded.

"I don't. And if it's all the same with you, I think I'd rather leave it that way."

"Well, if you're being more sociable these days, then why don't you join us for a drink this evening after your shift?"

"Don't look at me, I have to be there," Mike said as Tom shot him a glance.

"Love to," Tom said, snatching at his coffee and rising from the table. "Ladies," he offered, raising his cup, "I'll see you in ten then. I presume it's down to me to stock us up?"

CHAPTER TWENTY-SEVEN

Ethan lay awake in silence, arms rested behind his head, staring up into the nothingness of the darkness before him. It had been a condition that had been with him since he was a child and only worsened when forging a career for himself within his chosen field. A busy mind had been what his father had called it. In medical terms it was overactive brain circuitry that refused to let matters rest once his curiosity had piqued. As a young boy Ethan could stay awake through the night, initially wondering how his beloved Liverpool had fared in the evening fixture his parents had deemed too late to listen to on the radio, before playing the fixture out in full, seeing every pass, every goal, with unnerving accuracy. Through university and his late teens it had been the thought of girls, conversations they might share and dates they might go on, until his final year of course, when he had met Emily. From that moment on she had filled his every thought, and with her soothing influence and nightly comfort, Ethan had enjoyed the longest sustained period of nocturnal normality he had ever known. The arrival of Caitlin, coinciding with his newly formed association with the Met on an ongoing basis had seen him endure sleep deprivation, followed by a return to waking thoughts that still desperately needed to be answered. It was those myriad thoughts that swirled in a haze within him, searching for clarity.

"Just go to sleep," he said aloud, feeling the aches of every muscle asking him to switch off and succumb to the need for rest.

"*Has to be something, has to be something.*"

Growling at himself, Ethan threw the covers back and sat up, accepting defeat, before donning his dressing gown and quietly making his way downstairs.

As he headed down, Ethan could hear the sound of the percolator in action and was surprised at having to wince as he turned into the hallway due to the light already emanating from the kitchen. Abbey, dressed in thick pink cotton pyjamas, stood over the coffee machine drumming her fingers on the worktop, pressing from heel to toe, as if walking on the spot to keep her bare feet from standing on the cold flooring too long.

"You suck at being quiet." Abbey laughed. "You might as well have thrown yourself down the stairs."

"Sorry," Ethan said repentantly, slumping into a seat at the table.

"Coffee?"

"Caffeine's probably the last thing I need," he said, rubbing his sinuses and yawning. "Yes please."

"Couldn't sleep either then," Abbey said, placing a steaming mug of coffee in front of Ethan.

"Thanks. I know I'm missing something, we're missing something. It's there, burrowing away at the back of my mind. I just can't bring it to the fore. Why are you up?"

"That place. That's the worst I've ever seen," Abbey offered. "Every time I close my eyes, I can see it as if I'm back in the room, smell it, as if it were next to me. I can't believe I'm telling you this. It's embarrassing," she said uneasily.

"It's normal," Ethan replied. "I'd be more worried if you thought nothing of it."

"And on top of that, that bloody fingerprint. I thought we had the mistake."

"Maybe we do, maybe we don't. Just because we can't match it doesn't mean it was meant to be found," Ethan reasoned.

"One print. One print on the eggshell. Sounds planted to me. How do we know it even belongs to him? Some other poor sod might be missing a limb too," Abbey argued.

"May well be, or maybe he couldn't crack an egg with a glove on," Ethan proposed. "You can't torture yourself with hypotheticals, you'll be up all night," he continued, hiding a smile as he took an indulgent drink of the coffee.

"So take them out then," Abbey said, getting up from the table and pacing the kitchen, warming her hands on either side of her mug of coffee. "What are we left with?"

"Three bodies, two murders, time, patience and a lot of pride in what he does. They're not just replicas, they're perfect imitations. The two victims meet the standard requirement of being from the lower ebb of society," Ethan considered aloud.

"Allowing him the time. It's not that they won't be missed, it just takes longer," Abbey said rationally. "No way he could've known the young lad's parents had been looking for him for the last six months. He'd have just seen a runaway. Meadows met the parents yesterday. Homeless, half a mile from home. Why didn't he just go home? How are they supposed to live with that? Knowing he was within shouting distance."

"It's impassive. He does it because he wants to. Lives alone, maybe a girlfriend, but definitely not married. Needs to have that solitary life in order to free himself up. High intelligence, to the point of self-grandeur. The longer this goes on, the more personal gratification he'll experience. That's when the mistakes occur, when they get to the point they consider themselves omnipotent," Ethan vented, lost in his own thoughts.

"We still working on him being a doc, Doc?" Abbey asked, temporarily coming to a pause in her attempts to wear down the ceramic tiling.

"Medicine yes, not a doctor though, not a real one anyway," Ethan answered with a grin. "They're too accountable. It wouldn't offer the freedom of movement."

"Last time out he was seen, just by the wrong person. Who's to say we haven't got another eyewitness waiting to talk?" Abbey suggested.

"Of those apartments that have tenants, which are the minority, we have every one of them seeing and hearing nothing. Can't see that situation changing. Especially as the details make the papers. Would you offer information on someone like that?" Ethan asked.

"That was the drop-off, what about the collection?" Abbey asked. "We know the shelters he used, surely you stay local?"

"Come on then," Ethan said, getting to his feet.

"Now? It's nearly two in the morning."

"When all the homeless are as at home as they ever are."

"Can I at least change?" she asked, spreading her arms out to display her pyjamas in full.

"You can," Ethan answered as he made his way out of the kitchen and upstairs to do so himself.

"And I'm driving," Abbey called after him, topping up her mug with fresh coffee.

The satnav had stated that the journey was a little over twenty minutes, door to door. Clearly the virtual world didn't allow for the reality of London traffic which meant on any given weekday Abbey could expect to have been driving for closer to an hour.

As it was, with little to no traffic occupying the streets, at an hour when good, bad or indifferent, the majority of London's ever-growing population were asleep, she had managed it in just fifteen minutes. Abbey braked to a sudden stop, having slowed the car outside of the Shaftesbury Theatre, bracing herself against the jolt as Ethan banged his head which had been resting on the passenger window.

"Next time you can drive," she snapped.

"You said you wanted to," Ethan replied wearily, stretching, and wiping his eyes.

"Can't sleep in a comfy bed, but fifteen minutes in a car and you're away with the fairies."

"Works for a lot of families," Ethan said as he got out of the car, stretching his limbs further. "Used to have to take Caitlin out night after night if we wanted to get her off."

"It's fucking freezing too," she ranted.

"Just be glad you're not staying for the night, every night, then you'd know what cold is," Ethan said.

"Shall we then?" she said, crossing her arms tightly and looking down the length of the street, the darkness and inactivity broken by shadows flashing before them, elongated then shrinking, allowing no impression of where the movements were originating.

"You know why this street was built?" Ethan asked as they began pacing their way south down Shaftesbury Avenue. "To move the impoverished out of the city centre," he answered before being asked.

"You know a lot of crap," Abbey said, trying to force her mouth below the neckline of her coat, her mood lifting. "We ever enter The Highwayman's quiz, you're with us," she offered in a muffled tone. "So what are the rules?"

"Don't kick anyone to see if they are awake, or alive. And

don't complain about the cold whilst wearing a nice thick jacket."

"You're a funny guy. We're just going to walk then?" she asked.

"Pretty much. Anyone that looks our way, look them over, but don't stare. As we walk along, glance down each alleyway and opening, and if you see anyone, do the same thing. This time of night, we're the anomalous."

"The what?"

"The inconsistent, the abnormality. We're the ones that don't belong here," he explained. "You know the phrase *street smarts*?" he asked.

Abbey nodded.

"Well, they've got it in spades. If someone knows something, and they want to share, we won't need to be asking any questions."

They walked at a steady pace, attracting little attention as they passed by theatres that a handful of hours earlier would've been bustling with locals and tourists alike, heaping praise on another glorious performance as they made their way back to their hotels or homes within the city or surrounding counties. The line between a vibrant London evening and the eerie early hours was a fine one. As the last of the trains pulled out of Kings Cross, it was as if the entire city took its cue to fall into slumber, and a much darker mood filled the air. Ethan had returned the inquisitive looks of a couple of vagrants, both of whom had turned away into the shadows rather than attract further attention. Abbey had seen only those in search of sleep, filling the gaps between shop doorways along with any other superficial refuge that may provide some form of cover, keeping her head bowed as she walked. Some way ahead an obese outline staggered toward them, wavering, mumbling obscenities barely reaching them through the still air. Ethan threaded his arm through Abbey's, like a couple enjoying an evening stroll a little later than intended.

"Wonderful!" Abbey said, having looked down at Ethan's arm with surprise, and then seeing the man ahead.

"It's shut, it's all shut," he slurred, placing a hand on Ethan's shoulder.

"Just on our way home," Ethan replied, motioning past the man with Abbey as the smell of the man's nightly activities attacked their senses.

The drunken man clasped his hand tighter on Ethan's shoulder, planting him in place.

"Woah, woah, woah. You go when I say you go. I'll have your wallet, unless you want to pay in kind?" he cackled, grabbing at Abbey's crotch.

Abbey pulled away instinctively, and as the man reached further, his grip on Ethan's shoulder slackened, allowing him to thrust a flattened hand forward, driving his fingers into the drunkard's throat. The man crumpled to the ground in shock, holding a hand to his throat and gasping for air, feeling like he was trying to fill his lungs by sucking through a straw. Starting to retch, the man looked up searchingly at Abbey and Ethan, pleading and apprehensive, awaiting the follow-up.

"Well, aren't you full of surprises," Abbey said.

"Up you come," Ethan said with a resigned sigh, lifting him to his feet and leaning him forward from the waist as if he were trying to help him touch his toes.

"What are you doing?" Abbey asked. "We should be running him in, not helping him."

"In through the nose, out through the mouth. Deep breaths, nice and slow," Ethan said reassuringly. "Not sure that's going to achieve much," he said, turning to Abbey, "and I'm not sure Meadows would approve of our early morning stroll, do you?"

"Fine," she conceded. "Do we need to babysit him though?"

"Could've killed me," the drunken man mumbled, his breathing slowing.

"And now he's the victim. Fucking priceless," Abbey snapped, shaking her head and lifting him to his full height with a jolt, causing the man to cower and brace in anticipation of another hit.

"What do you think you're doing?" a voice shouted from down the street.

Abbey and Ethan turned to see another homeless resident walking with purpose toward them with a length of heavy piping in his right hand.

"Two of you this time then," he continued as he advanced on them.

"Bingo," Ethan said softly.

"Back the fuck off him," the man barked, as he came into the light of the streetlamps. He was well built, around thirty years of age, and as well groomed as a homeless individual could manage, a look of fierce determination focused entirely on Ethan and Abbey as he persisted along his set path without slowing.

"What do you mean 'this time'?" Abbey asked in an even tone.

The man deliberated for the first time since making himself apparent, perplexed reasoning replacing the adrenaline that had fuelled in preparation for action.

"You were expecting someone else?" Ethan offered. "This is Detective Swift. My name's Ethan Marshall. We're trying to find out if anyone saw anything two nights ago. Someone who didn't belong, maybe leaving with company?"

"Like you two," the man said.

"Can leave with us if he wants," Abbey said to the drunkard whilst retrieving her badge from within her jacket and showing it to the man before them.

"Probably not too dissimilar," Ethan reasoned, nodding at Abbey.

"Do not try that crap again," she said softly into their attacker's ear. "Go home."

"Fuck you," the man said, shuffling off, heading nowhere.

"Tactful," Ethan said.

"I didn't mean..." Abbey began to explain before giving up on the idea.

"Want to get a hot drink, something to eat?" Ethan asked.

"You offering the same menu Stewart was offered? You know anywhere open at this time?" the man countered, gripping the piping tighter.

"Station," Abbey proposed.

"We're good here," he said.

"Did you know Stewart?" Ethan asked.

"He was a good kid. I'd speak to him at the shelter if I saw him. He found it tough you know. Some can adapt, others..."

"And you saw who he went off with?" Abbey asked.

"Saw him, heard him, didn't recognise him. You know how often fortune favours the homeless," he said, pausing. "It doesn't. I knew something wasn't right. But I just pulled the blanket around me and looked after number one."

"Understandable. Attract no attention, you attract no trouble," Ethan said. "So you saw what the guy looked like?"

"I had a family you know. The job, the car, the house, wife. Lost it all. Found her with another guy in our house, our home. That was it, I just walked away. Never went back to work, never went back home. Too much pride. Showed her didn't I? My dad used to say you can take away everything a man has, but he will still have his dignity. Well, I gave that away on a plate when I attracted no attention," he said, choking on the lump in his throat as tears welled.

"So help us now," Abbey pleaded. "This guy doesn't care about people's dignity."

"Didn't look like he was capable. One of those trench coat mafia types. Tall and skinny, long, matted, greasy black hair, pale as you like. Like a ghost in clothing. Too keen. You saw the change, just briefly, when Stewart said he wasn't interested. That flash of anger. That's when I should've stepped in. That's..."

"How old would you say he was?"

"Erm, twenty-one, twenty-two. Would've liked to have seen him try that shit with me. He studied the pack and picked off the weakest. How cowardly is that? That's it, then they were gone. Fuck!" he yelled, throwing the piping down the alleyway, breaking the sound of the night as it bounced off metal and rolled to a stop somewhere in the darkness.

"You sure you don't want that drink and dinner at the station?" Abbey offered.

"My reward for my good deed for the day? A little late don't you think? Thanks, but I'd rather go and see if the ground might open up for me somewhere."

A silence fell as they watched him walk away with shoulders slouched, bearing the weight of a heavy conscience and multiple what-ifs. Abbey and Ethan held their ground until he turned down an alleyway and out of sight. Ethan tugged at Abbey's sleeve and started the trek back to the car, the adrenaline fading away, replaced by every muscle suddenly screaming for respite and the blissful shutdown only sleep could bring.

They had walked the length of the return without conversation, both unscrambling their thoughts, both tired.

"Twenty-two, twenty-three," Abbey said, turning the engine over, waiting for the spark of life to allow them to start the journey home.

"*Twenty-one, twenty-two,* he said. But I heard."

"That's two from two."

"Tall and skinny is hardly average height, average build though."

"You think we've got more than one?"

"I don't know. I do know I'm not prepared to say I'm wrong just yet. Call it male pride," Ethan said drowsily, resting his head on the passenger side window.

"Call it arrogance," Abbey said with a smirk as she pulled out onto the empty carriageway.

CHAPTER TWENTY-EIGHT

Superintendent Meadows was bristling with rage as he slammed the phone down on his desk, looking over at his lead detective and criminologist, both barely able to keep their eyes open. With a disapproving shake of the head he spun his chair to face away from them, looking up at Vince Lombardi, who in turn was studying the deserted gridiron playing field before him in one of Meadows' most coveted black-and-white pictures.

"Big night was it?" Meadows asked pointedly.

"Of sorts," Abbey snapped. "We got a face to put with that fingerprint."

"What?" Meadows said, spinning round to face them both.

"Of sorts," Ethan repeated dryly, looking at Abbey. "We got an eyewitness who gave a description, a good one, of the person the fingerprint probably belongs to."

"When was this? I checked the logs. No one came in last night."

"They didn't come in," Abbey stated.

"You want to expand on that?"

"We went down to Shaftesbury Avenue," she continued, awaiting the repercussion.

"Off duty. Alone. I'm guessing no one else knew of your whereabouts."

"No, sir."

"Can't sleep again then, Ethan?" Meadows asked matter-of-factly, an exasperated glance from one to the other. "It's not like it was, Ethan. There's protocol that needs to be followed. And swanning off on a goose hunt isn't covered. However successful it might prove to be."

"You thought I was drunk. We were drunk. I say we put this whole horrible mess behind us and concentrate on what's important," Ethan suggested, feigning offence and pausing for effect. "Can your beloved Packers really win the Super Bowl this year?"

Abbey spat out a laugh.

"I only thought you were drunk because it takes you two drinks to get there!" Meadows said, simply shaking his head.

"You know what they're calling him do you? The Property Market Killer. The chief super has told me in no uncertain terms, that should we not make a breakthrough soon, then I shall be held personally accountable for the current economic climate and stagnation of the London property market."

"Seems a little strong," Abbey commented.

"People are going to be scared to sell their houses, Abbey. So, while I am immeasurably frustrated with your actions, I am willing to put that irritation to one side and hear all about your exciting little escapade. And yes, Ethan, the Packers can of course claim number six. Winning is habit."

"Unfortunately so is losing," Ethan countered.

"And that is what we are doing right now. We're trailing and heading into the fourth quarter. Throw me an audible."

"I have no idea what you two are on about. We do, however, have a description of a tall, greasy, early-twenties perp."

"Contradicts what our other witness offered. We happy with this? Ethan?"

"Would've been happier with a corroboration, but seems genuine. Which gives us three possible scenarios."

"Three?" Abbey asked.

"It's either the same person, described differently or using disguises, two different people entirely working together, or part of a network whereby we don't know how many might be involved."

"Do we have reason to think it might be part of a grander operation?" Meadows asked warily.

"Only that the doc isn't happy with kids committing the crimes."

"Absolutely right I'm not," Ethan said defensively. "All logic would say the lad from the Bundy copy saw somebody from the shadows he was hiding in, and without a clear view, settled on them being average in every way, right down to the most common brown hair. Meaning we use the most recent description as the gospel according to Swift. And while I don't dispute its relevance, if this kid is as young as described, then he's not unaided. The planning alone requires someone of greater experience. The patience wouldn't be prevalent in someone of that age. I'm telling you, we're looking for someone in their mid to late thirties. Plus, a young man goes against the medical background."

"Okay, Okay. Can we get a sketch out there of this guy?"

"If we can find the witness. Would be another door-to-door, if you'll pardon the pun," Abbey answered.

"Fine. You do what you've got to do here, then you get back out with the artist. God knows he won't want to be dragged in here. We do this where he's most comfortable. And Ethan, get off and see your little girl for the weekend. We're not going to see miracles overnight here, so she may as well get to hug her daddy. And I've a feeling he could do with one himself."

"Thank you," Ethan mouthed silently as he and Abbey exited the superintendent's office.

"You always got to be right?" Abbey asked as they made their way through the corridors to her office.

"Not got to be," Ethan replied with a smirk.

"Really," Abbey said, picking up the pace until she arrived at her office and threw herself into her chair, looking up at Ethan.

"It's a blessing as much as a curse. Honestly, once you start being right so often..."

"So you've never been wrong?"

"I wouldn't say never. There was one time when I thought I was wrong, and I was actually right. So I guess I was wrong then!"

"Ethan," Abbey snapped, sitting up and leaning on her desk.

"Abbey," he replied in the same exaggerated tone. "You know I'm only joking. Of course I've been wrong. Plenty of times. Too many times. And this is maybe another, but something's telling me it's not."

"I thought you'd be a man of science. Not someone to go on gut instinct."

"They don't need to be exclusive of each other. A gut feeling normally has some science behind it. You can break it all down to atoms and chemicals if you really want to," Ethan offered.

Abbey buried her head in her hands, rubbing at her eyes and moving on to her temples as her head hung heavy, keeping her eyes closed.

"What would you give for a little space?" the gruff voice of

Jameson asked, breaking the silence and causing Abbey to raise her weary head.

"Anything," Abbey said, shooting Ethan a look before breaking into a smile.

"Exactly," Jameson said, walking into the office and placing his trilby on Abbey's desk. No sooner had it hit the surface when Abbey picked it up and pulled it on tight, her tresses framing her face from underneath it. Ethan stared a little too long, catching Abbey's eyeline as she looked for a reflection, turning his attention to Pat Jameson as a self-imposed distraction.

"Really?" Jameson asked pointedly, addressing his mentee.

"Until the day you retire."

Jameson puffed out his cheeks and shook his head, turning back to Ethan.

"Not my toughest extraction ever."

"The husband," Ethan offered resignedly.

"The husband. Cost him a broken nose though."

Abbey's head shot back from admiring her new look, wide-eyed at Jameson.

"Not me. He started explaining that his missus cracked him one. Like she turned on a tap! She's with him now though."

"He mean it?" Ethan asked.

"Seems not. Do they ever? They were arguing over him and the daughter not having enough space. How could they think of having a family when they never had time to themselves et cetera? Verbals exchanged that carried on upstairs, then apparently she questioned whether he was good enough for her daughter in the first place. He pushed her in frustration, and she hit her head on the doorframe."

"You believe him?" Abbey asked.

"Tech boys support it. Found residue of blood underneath

cleaning fluids on the doorframe, and traces on the floor. Single blow suggests he didn't beat on her afterwards."

"And his lame-arse attempt at covering his tracks?" Abbey asked.

"Just that. He remembered seeing the reports in the paper and the only ones he could remember from school were Jack the Ripper and the Boston Strangler."

"Good choice then," Ethan interjected.

"No kidding," Abbey said.

"Anyway, barring a bathtub and a stocking, he was guessing."

"Badly," Abbey added.

"He wasn't to know our copycat was quite so meticulous. Panic clouded judgement. His attempts at distraction only focused the attention. No way our man would make the mistake, or settle for a pair of tights over a stocking," Ethan surmised.

"Actions, reactions and consequences. Three lives changed forever in a split second," Jameson concluded. "Wasn't quite the pleasurable experience I was after."

"At least you finish your cases," Abbey suggested.

"Patience is also a form of action," Jameson said with a soft smile as he lifted the trilby gently from Abbey's head.

"Wait for the mistake," Abbey considered under her breath. "So you on for a long weekend too then?"

"If I stop, I'll stop," Jameson replied. "Domestic battery for me," he continued as he stepped out of the office with a cursory wave.

"Right then," Abbey said, getting to her feet, "I'm going to go and grab the least repressed wannabe artist we have and find our witness. Enjoy your weekend, Ethan."

"I will. Good luck with the search," he said.

"I'll see you at home on Monday," she said as she made her

way round her desk and kissed him affectionately on the cheek like numerous other halves around the country as they take their leave for the daily grind.

"Give Caitlin a hug from me," Abbey said as she hastily made her exit, leaving Ethan standing in the empty office space feeling slightly confused.

CHAPTER TWENTY-NINE

He'd been thinking about it for the last couple of days. Having read the various reports across all the major dailies, alongside the more detailed articles within the local city press purporting the grim reality of the situation gripping the capital, he had decided he was a fan of the double-entendre moniker with which he had been labelled. A clever little title given the current climate. No doubt thought up by one of tomorrow's brilliant young minds who would see none of the credit for his insightfulness. Given the choice, would the greater powers of the London representatives rather see the Property Market Killer, the individual, brought to justice, or the economic executioner seen off and the green shoots continuously promised finally starting to show? Even though it be from his own hand, the thought that every single person in power, if pushed, would choose for economic growth saddened Tom a little.

Coming off the back of a double shift, Tom was glad to be within the cocoon of his apartment. A demanding workload had always reaped the rewards of providing the spontaneous highs of people passing from the world, laid before him, a gift needing no arrangement or personal involvement, and had always been something he had cherished. But ever since agreeing to go out for drinks and muted conversation with Mike and his faction of hospice employees, the idea that they were now friends, and the pretence of holding such a façade, had left him physically drained.

He had been out of the shower for over an hour but continued to pace the apartment, air con on full, the image of the crazed psychopath from too many films playing on his mind. He remembered watching Buffalo Bill doing much the same thing, in between finding the time to abduct young women, and then skinning them. Tom had been seventeen when he first watched what was now considered to be a modern classic, rooting for escape rather than capture, unsure of why the supposed antagonist courted his empathy so readily.

"Now it places the lotion in the basket," he said aloud, downing a tall glass of milk and then refilling it to the brim before moving naturally through to his study, hand rock-steady, the drink motionless.

Fully clothed and sat at his PC, Reed flicked from his watch to the clock on the bottom-right of his computer screen.

Ten thirty. So where the fuck is he? he thought.

Reed had filled his own busy day by spending his hard-earned benefits, dropping his washing off at his mother's, and spending the last eight and a half hours eradicating the virtual earth of alien invasion and all torture and misery that accompany such an incursion.

Having made the transition from console to workstation he drummed his fingers next to the mouse, eyes flicking over to the flawless image of an unidentifiable creature in mid-explosion, internal organs becoming external.

Sniggering to himself, he turned his attention back to the private messenger screen before him, typing once more.

Any danger?

The letters sat small on the empty canvas, the icon blinking, imploring additional scripture. Reed looked back over to the frozen screen, the controller calling to him from its restful position on the arm of the chair. Bouncing his foot, he stared hard at the screen, willing it to respond. With nothing forthcoming he stood with a tut and pushed the chair forcefully under the unit. As he did so the response from Tutor filtered through, ten thirty-four.

My apologies.
    Punctuality was your requirement, Reed replied instantly.
    It was indeed, and for my indiscretion I apologise.

Ground rules had been laid, and that the pupil was keen to enforce them was reassuring. He had been let down twice already. Trust was to be earned and would no longer be issued so freely. That planning and implementation matter bode well for his latest recruit.

I can only speak of my admiration for the accuracy with which you fulfilled your role with the undesirable, Tutor enthused.
    The sick shit's your thing. Just tell me where and when, Reed submitted.

Emotion wasn't going to be an issue either. This young man showed none. He liked the definitiveness of it all. Power was important to him, but so too was control. It was comforting to know he was working with a psychopath rather than having to deal with the potential unpredictability of a sociopath. Tom cracked his neck from side to side with a satisfied inhalation, taking a long swig of milk as the next conversation flashed through.

How many others you got involved? Reed enquired.
We are now a party of two. Some are not best equipped for the mission. Sadly, men are needed where boys were unable. He must now solve his own predicament, and for that he and his mother may well pay the price. Alas, I digress. I merely wished to convey my gratitude. When we are ready to progress I will be in touch once more.
Where and when? Reed asked again. *That it?*

The icon blinked, unresponsive for several seconds, before Reed decided nothing more would be imminent and withdrew himself back into the world of planetary saviour, walking away from his personal chat room in the same carefree manner as a teenager logging off from their social networking addiction having discussed the homework assignment due the following day.

Tom watched the blinking icon, allowing time to pass before declaring the conversation ended. While his newest disciple, if he could even be considered that, may never be what he might term to be a friend, he believed for the first time that a partner had been unearthed. Tom exited the study, stifling a yawn, taking the empty glass with him and placing it in the dishwasher containing a solitary plate and knife and fork and set the appliance to run a full wash. Looking over the pristine surfaces, Tom afforded himself a satisfied nod before turning off the lights and leaving the low hum of electrical activity to run its course as he retired for the night.

CHAPTER THIRTY

Ethan had arrived back in the very early hours, tired from the journey and mentally exhausted from spending that time micro-analysing every detail that may yet prove to be as significant as it could insignificant. Resting his head on the front door of the place he had called home for the last five years, he quietly slid the key into the lock and clicked it over, entering in near silence. Standing in the darkened hallway, a weight felt like it had been lifted simply by coming home. The comfort of belonging, and knowing that family were just thirteen steps away, caught sharp in Ethan's throat as he swallowed hard and fought against the urge of racing up the stairs and taking his little girl in his arms, both to protect her from the world as he knew it, and to convince himself that there was far better within it than he endured so habitually. Stepping through to the lounge Ethan looked over the row of pictures resting atop the fireplace of Emily with Caitlin as a baby and then the annual pictures insisted upon by Nana. She had always said it was important to show Caitlin how much she'd grown, and to illustrate to Ethan just how quickly they grew up, ensuring he be thankful for every minute he had with her. Ethan fell back onto the settee and closed his eyes, knowing sleep would come easy tonight, he wanted to be there waiting when Caitlin came down for breakfast in the morning.

It had reached seven fifteen when Ethan was awoken with a start as the breath was knocked from him with Caitlin throwing her small frame on top of his resting body and wrapping her arms tightly around his neck, pushing her cheek next to his and squeezing tight.

"Daddy!" she squealed in delight.

"Hey, Trouble," Ethan replied groggily, wrapping his arms around her, absorbing her affection.

"I'm not trouble, you're trouble."

A gentle breeze of cold air drifted through the archway leading to the kitchen, wafting the instant hunger-inducing smells of fried bread, eggs and bacon into the surrounding air. Caitlin lifted her head sharply as the bacon started to sizzle.

"Piggyback?" she asked excitedly.

Ethan blew into Caitlin's face suddenly and as she closed her eyes and scrambled a delayed hand barrier, he swung her round onto his back, and lifting himself from the sofa, carried her through to the kitchen where Nana was busy shuffling three pans at once, while vigilantly keeping an eye on the overly aggressive toaster to her right.

"I thought only teenagers slept fully clothed after a drunken night out," she proclaimed, not turning.

"Teenagers and somnolent professors," Ethan answered as he retrieved the orange juice from the fridge and poured two glasses and a beaker to accompany the ensuing breakfast spread.

Nana popped the toaster and threw the two slices into a pan, then dished up the other bits and pieces onto a single plate and presented it like a waitress seeing out her days in an American diner.

"Order up," she shouted as she placed the plate before him.

"Order up," Caitlin repeated excitedly.

"Thanks," Ethan said, tucking in.

"Nice to have you home," Nana said, kissing the top of his head, "and one French toast on its way for madam."

"I don't want French toast, I want eggy bread," Caitlin countered.

"As you wish, although it'll mean me starting all over again," Nana conceded with a theatrical sigh, and knowing smile in Ethan's direction.

Caitlin gave Nana a serious look, pondering her next move as Nana placed her hands on her hips and held Caitlin's inquisitive stare. Ethan took a sip of his orange juice and gave a wink to Caitlin.

"I want eggy bread," she said with a giggle.

Nana gave a look of defeat before flashing a smile, sending Caitlin into even greater giggles, and turning to finish off the final frying pan of the breakfast.

Having finished breakfast, Ethan had taken great pleasure in simply being able to be a dad with no other commitments or distractions. After bathing Caitlin, along with her dolls, Daisy, Kathy and Mo, he had allowed Caitlin to choose what she would like to wear for the day. Once Caitlin had been talked out of going outside in wellies, knickers and a bobble hat, she had made the desperately difficult decision of how she would like to spend the day with Dad and Nana.

"Flingos," she called out.

Flingos had been her nickname for flamingos ever since she had struggled with the pronunciation when she was younger.

She had been captivated by them from the moment she saw them. Perfectly balancing on one leg and bright pink, her eyes widening at the explanation of how they had got their colour, and then laughing hysterically at the potential image had they changed their diet to other foods suggested by Ethan.

They had spent the day in glorious sunshine walking leisurely amongst the crowds of Linton Zoo, being sure to take in the sights of each and every quarter of the park. Caitlin proudly announced which species they were looking at as Nana and Ethan followed a few paces behind each time. Ethan had made a point of engaging Caitlin in the finer details of the information provided, asking her about where they were from and what they might eat were they in their natural habitat. Nana had enjoyed taking a back seat in proceedings and watching her doting son-in-law enjoying the time with her granddaughter. As the sun began to set and the park emptied as quickly as it had been occupied hours earlier, Ethan cradled an exhausted Caitlin back to the car, letting her doze peacefully, sucking her thumb and drawing numerous looks of indulgence from those around them. As Ethan placed her in the back of the car his phone vibrated, causing her to stir just a little.

"Are you going to answer that?" Nana asked as they both buckled up for the journey.

"It can wait until we get home," he said softly as he started the engine, checking Caitlin in the rear-view mirror.

"She can't always be the only woman in your life, you know."

"Maria," Ethan groaned.

"I'm just saying. You can't hold on to the past forever."

"I just feel..."

"Well don't," Maria interrupted. "Guilt is for when you've

done something wrong. And you've done nothing wrong. Don't ever forget that, Ethan."

Ethan sighed heavily, a half smile in Nana's direction as the phone vibrated once more.

"Saved by the bell," she said. "You want to take it?"

"I'll call them when we get home. Twenty minutes won't make a difference."

"And this old woman will stop harassing you. I just want you to be happy, Ethan."

"I know," he said with a crooked smile.

Ethan had taken Caitlin straight up to bed and having managed to get her changed against her tired resistance, pressed redial as he made his way back down to the lounge. Maria smiled fondly and motioned an empty cup to her mouth, which Ethan gladly accepted with a silent nod as the ringing began at the other end.

"You called?" Ethan said as the phone was answered.

"Hey, what's up, Doc? You have a good day?"

"Sunshine, animals, and crime-free. I can't complain. You?"

"Ah, you worried I'm getting bored without you?" Abbey asked cheekily.

"Erm..." he said hesitantly.

"Don't worry, Ethan, Lucy has kept me company. We've even managed to find time for a weekend."

"I take it that means you got your artist's impression."

"Indeed it does. You think I'd be at home now if I hadn't?"

"Tell me," he said resignedly.

"Long black hair, greasy, pale, all in black. Narrow features, eyes look like they're too close to each other. Why is that the case with criminals? Younger than you'd like him to be basically," she posed in an even tone.

"So you called to irk me?" Ethan responded sardonically.

"I apologise if you feel irked. That was never my intent."

"Uh-huh."

"I actually called because Lucy had a visitor this morning, so to speak. And thinks he may be of interest."

"Another one?"

"Only a possible. She's going in tomorrow for a more in-depth appraisal."

"You need me there tomorrow," Ethan said through a sigh.

"No, no. Spend the weekend with your little girl. We can catch the highlights Monday morning. Meet me there?"

"Sounds like a plan. Thanks, Abbey."

"Tschüss," she said, clicking off.

Ethan frowned at the mobile in his hand, smiling to himself at the sign-off.

"She sounds pretty," Maria mused, handing Ethan a cup of tea and taking a seat.

"Really, and you could hear her from the kitchen could you?"

"Didn't need to. I heard you. Your voice rises a pitch."

"Does it?" Ethan said indifferently.

"Always has. Even after you'd been with Emily all those years. When she walked through the door, or if she called, you'd go up an octave. Endearing really. Tell me about her," Maria said.

CHAPTER THIRTY-ONE

Ethan pulled up alongside Abbey's Fiat mid-yawn, and gave a cursory wave. Abbey nodded in response as she finished off her mobile breakfast, an eclectic mixture of Costa coffee, white, two sugars, a banana, and a granola bar. Caffeine and sugar, just what Ethan needed. At eight o'clock in the morning, the car park was still sparsely populated, unopposed vehicles sat alone dotted across the gravelled landscape. Why didn't they park outside the front of the building? It wasn't far enough to pass as exercise. Ethan assumed it was simply human nature. Over time you found "your" parking space, and whether the car park was full or deserted, that was where you parked. Abbey clambered out of the driver side door, wrestling her bag over her head whilst trying to not spill the coffee and holding the brunch bar in her mouth.

"You look exhausted," she said through a mouthful of oaty nutrition.

Ethan stifled a further yawn and ran his fingers across his eyes, pinching at the bridge of his nose. "I just don't remember having so much energy when I was a kid."

"Tough weekend?"

"As much as the zoo tired her out, the Disney marathon reinvigorated her."

"Disney marathon?" Abbey asked, intrigued.

"Oh yeah, I must've sung the entire back catalogue yesterday."

"And you knew the words to all these classics?"

"I'd love to say it's because we've got the sing-along versions..."

"But you don't even look at the screen," Abbey said, laughing and shaking her head. "A man of many levels, Doc."

"Shall we?" Ethan suggested, gesturing in the direction of the morgue.

Abbey shrugged and headed off. "The circle of life," she said back over her shoulder with a grin.

"Wow, you look rough, heavy night?" Lucy said, welcoming them as they entered from the corridor.

"Seems to be the general consensus," Ethan replied.

"Disney," Abbey answered as if giving a logical explanation.

"Uh-huh. Anyway..." Lucy said, turning her attention to the body on the tabletop.

The naked cadaver of Danny Jemson lay atop the autopsy tablet. The chest cavity had been prised open, and the stiffened skin walls stood without support, displaying an empty void where the functionality of life had been performed. The majority of the internal examination had been completed and was in the process of being put back together. The inner organs had all been weighed, tissue samples had been taken and now they sat collectively in a transparent bag waiting to be returned to their rightful residence.

"Wanna take the walk round?" Lucy asked as she began packing the open cavity with a woollen substance.

Abbey picked a pair of disposable gloves from the open box at the side of the room, tossing a second set to Ethan as she began to walk the body, visibly shuddering as she went past the bag of organs, and refocusing on the body itself.

Ethan hadn't moved and rather was watching fixated as Lucy continued to pack the core of the body with white fibre.

"It's called body packing," she said, carrying on with her work. "You've never seen it before?"

"Not the zip-up stage," he replied.

"Well, you see that bag of organs. That bag that doesn't leak?"

Ethan nodded.

"Guess what?"

"They leak," Abbey joined in as she took a closer look at bruising around the neck of the subject matter.

"Like a tap in an Eastern European hostel," Lucy explained, "so, seeing as we don't want fluid escaping onto the individual's clothing or the shiny new coffin lining they've paid so much for, we pack the body. Any seepage is then absorbed and held way past burial or cremation."

Ethan looked satisfied with the detailed tutorial and took to pacing the body himself while Abbey stood at the neck waiting for him to complete his circuit.

"And you think this is one of ours?" Ethan asked.

"He's got potential," Lucy said with a knowing smile.

"Strangulation?" Abbey asked aloud.

"Heavy bruising. He'd have been sore, but he didn't die of asphyxiation."

Ethan tilted his head, waiting for Lucy to elaborate.

"There aren't any other markings on him," Abbey reasoned.

"Not to the untrained eye," Lucy said in mock exasperation.

Abbey and Ethan looked to each other in acceptance of the challenge laid before them and took up position either side of the body, bending low and examining from the neck downwards.

"Cold, colder, freezing," Lucy commentated as they moved along the deceased to his feet.

"Why not just tell us, you witch!" Abbey snapped.

"I don't get company often. Not those that offer much in terms of conversation anyway. Are you really going to deny me my fun?" Lucy said in a soft tone.

"Fine," Abbey said, marching to the top of the body, looking down at Ethan by the dead man's feet watching the scene play out in front of him.

"Scorching," Lucy offered over-enthusiastically.

Shaking her head with derision, Abbey analysed the head, feeling round the back of the neck, feeling nothing but the handiwork of her friend's reconstruction. Sighing with frustration, Abbey lowered herself to have a clear view of the shoulders and neck, her knees instantly wanting to be relieved of the pressure placed upon them as she knelt on the uneven floor tiling.

Abbey frowned. "What's your marker pen for?" she said, looking at a small circular etching behind Danny Jemson's right ear.

"We have a winner," Lucy announced as Ethan moved hastily from one end of the corpse to the other to inspect the findings for himself, "and would the good doctor like to tell me the answer?"

"It's a puncture wound, a hypodermic?" he offered, joining Abbey's knelt position and trying to obtain the most accessible viewpoint.

"Indeed it is. And would you like to place a bet on what the substance was?"

Ethan looked from Lucy to Abbey, both suppressing smiles, as Abbey raised her hands in a *don't look at me* fashion.

Ethan stood, deep in concentration, recalling crimes of the past and any drugs of note, though that was far from a strong area of expertise for him. He shook his head, irritated to not make the connection.

"A clue for our expert," Lucy said, accentuating on the word 'expert' with air quotes. "Who is considered to be the most prolific serial killer in our country's history?"

"Diamorphine," Ethan concluded.

"Diamorphine," Lucy repeated, "and a lot of it too. Kid this size didn't stand a chance. Like I said, he has potential."

"What?" Abbey asked pointedly, looking to either of her colleagues for a layman's explanation.

"Harold Shipman used diamorphine as his weapon of choice. In simple terms it induces coma. His victims were generally of an age where natural causes were accepted as the foundation of bereavement, which is why he was able to prolong his actions for such a length of time," Ethan explained.

"So he could be one of ours?" Abbey posed.

"I don't think we can rule it out. Though it doesn't fit the pattern," Ethan answered.

"He's a famous serial killer isn't he?" Lucy asked.

"Infamous," Ethan corrected, with a cheeky smile displaying his dimple, "but not revered. He certainly lacks the notoriety, the allure of the macabre."

"Maybe he's getting as bored with our lack of progress as I am," Abbey chipped in sarcastically.

"Or it goes back to our original crime scene," Ethan supposed.

"That wasn't even a murder," Lucy scoffed.

Abbey nodded knowingly. "To serve a purpose. But if that's true, it means he probably knew his victim. The copy, however lame it may be, kept his authenticity," she said, walking to the end of the table and reading the tag loosely hooked over the big toe of the deceased's left foot. "We just need to know who Danny Jemson was."

The silence that fell as all three in attendance pondered the open-ended question was short-lived as a rap on the swing doors preceded a heavily-breathing Pat Jameson making his entrance.

"Morning, all," he said breathlessly, removing his hat and spinning it in front of him.

"Hey, Irish," Ethan replied.

"What, like the whisky?" Lucy rationalised.

"Like the whisky," Abbey mimicked churlishly.

"And may I ask what your interest is with my suspect?" Jameson asked in his most authoritative tone.

"Your suspect? We're thinking our victim," Abbey responded.

"And you?" Jameson asked Ethan.

"Looking very possible."

Jameson sucked his teeth and walked slowly round the body, leaning in for a closer look every now and again and then readdressed his audience after a complete lap.

"The battery case I was looking at. Turns out it's more a case of attempted murder. The girl's on support at the hospital. Could go either way. They're just waiting to see which way she turns. Anyway, her friends say we shouldn't be looking any further than one Danny Jemson. Ex-boyfriend of ill repute according to her flatmates. Didn't take the break-up well. No signs of forced entry, no defensive wounds. If it were a marriage, we'd already have the spouse in custody. But..." he said, turning to the naked form of Danny Jemson, "as a suspect, he makes a better victim."

"Could be both," Ethan theorised. "Could be these girls just didn't like him."

"Them and someone else," Abbey said.

"All very interesting," Lucy cut in, "and while I would love to theorise with you, some of us still have work to finish," she said, looking back toward the bag of packing material.

"How'd you want to play it?" Jameson asked.

"He's viable in both scenarios until proven otherwise," Ethan surmised. "We need to know everything about Danny Jemson immediately."

"I'm on it," Abbey said, taking her leave, already dialling on her mobile as she pushed through the doors.

"Immediately could take some time," Jameson suggested. "Want to see what he may or may not have been involved in?"

"Why not. Until a distinction can be made, our cases are one and the same."

"Bye, boys," Lucy called out, concentrating on packing the body once more as Ethan and Jameson strode out with a sense of renewed purpose.

CHAPTER THIRTY-TWO

Assault and battery, just another case of domestic abuse in the heart of the city. Considering how the preceding events had actually led up to the poor girl's current situation, Tom couldn't think of a better outcome as far as an official enquiry was concerned. That's not to say he wouldn't prefer to knock the plug off the ventilation machine from the wall when leaving after his evening visit, but with the eyes of authority looking in a different direction, there seemed little reasoning for such a risk. Tom stood outside the young woman's private room, his face inches from the Plexiglas so that each breath temporarily steamed up the view, then cleared again with every inhalation. The old man assigned seemed to be simply seeing his time out on the force, asking the expected questions, making the usual promise of offering false hope to the nearest and dearest in justice being served accordingly. No doubt he'd seen more exciting times on the force, Tom considered, although he was surprised to be asked to make himself available once more for questions.

Rounds were being carried out. The latest set of interns following the less than enthusiastic senior medic like a congregation before the messiah himself, their dreams still intact of being the doctors of tomorrow and going on to greatness by curing the 'big C' or, even better, finding some new terminal illness and having their name put to it. Tom watched as they huddled around the end of the bed of a patient who would be seeing out her few remaining days within the confines of not only the hospital, but of the bed itself. The senior doctor described her debilitating condition in overt detail, graphically portraying what the old lady was to endure over the next week, or two, should she be unfortunate enough to have the strength to continue fighting, his tone clear, and loud enough for all passing traffic and fellow incumbents to hear. However great the doctor may envisage himself, sensitivity was not an asset. Tom slowly shook his head as he turned away from the hospital's perception of an education system where the young minds are provided with knowledge at the simple cost of a patient's self respect. As he did so, he caught sight of the detective who had introduced himself as Jameson, walking along the ward, only this time he was flanked by two younger contemporaries. Jameson gave a jovial wave as he caught Tom's eyeline, who returned a perfunctory nod of acknowledgement as the gap between them lessened.

"Mr Lindon, thanks for taking the time," Jameson said, proffering a handshake. "This is DI Swift, and Mr Ethan Marshall."

"A pleasure," Tom said, accepting all the extended hands in sequence.

"I was telling them how you were the first on scene, how she wouldn't even have made it this far without you."

"More down to my partner's abandonment of speed restrictions than anything I did," Tom replied with a smile.

"Too modest," Jameson said, shaking his head. "How's she doing?"

"Fighting, no improvement, but no deterioration as yet."

"Did you see anything on the way to the call, or anyone?" Abbey asked.

Tom shook his head, as if trying to recall the scene. "Can't think why anyone would've been out that night."

Ethan moved up to the Plexiglas divide, watching the pump forcing Susan's lungs to inflate, a mass of tubes supporting the life of a once healthy body. Her face still showed bruising, now a blend of deep purple and black contusions. Ethan sighed heavily, knowing that for every bit as bad as the front looked, it was from behind that the real damage had been inflicted.

"Who would do this?" he said softly.

"Some clown," Tom countered, joining Ethan at the screen, shaking his head and looking up at the corner of the ageing wooden framing, flaking above Ethan's head.

The swarm of interns swept through the four stationary bodies, obliviously creating a corridor of their own as they blindly followed their inspirational leader.

"The exuberance of youth," Jameson commented.

"With a god complex," Abbey quipped, drawing a scornful look from Ethan and Tom, although one carried far more weight than the other.

"You file reports don't you? After every call?" Abbey asked.

"We do," Tom confirmed. "Why is that relevant?"

"Well, if we can get your detailed report, then we won't need to be disturbing the victim while she is in such a restful state."

"She's unresponsive," Tom countered.

"For now," Abbey replied. "You have to do the reports that night, right? So recollections will be fresh, won't they?" Abbey said pointedly.

Tom sniffed, looked down at the floor and then back up, addressing Abbey alone.

"They will be, yes. Though I can save you the bother. Blunt force to the back of the head, found unconscious, multiple stab wounds on the back, through clothing, jagged blade. What do you call it?" he said, pausing for effect. "A crime of passion?"

"Still wouldn't mind seeing that report," Abbey said calmly.

"No problem, everything's filed nightly with records," Tom replied in a steady tone.

"Thanks, Mr Linden, appreciate that. I'll arrange a copy for collection. Sorry to have kept you. I'm sure your partner will be keen to start his shift," Jameson said, lightly offering a concluding handshake which was readily accepted.

"Mr Marshall," Tom said, excusing himself with a nod, ignoring Abbey and making his way across the ward, heading for the elevators and access to the lower levels of the hospice.

"How rude!" Abbey declared.

"You're not wrong," Jameson said. "What was with the dressing-down?"

"I don't like him. 'More down to my partner's abandonment of speed restrictions'," she said, mimicking. "He lapped it up."

"Ethan?" Jameson said, exasperated, looking for support.

"Sorry to disappoint you, Pat. But he knows more than he's giving up. When I asked who could do such a thing..."

"'Some clown'. Is he wrong?" Jameson interrupted.

"Up and to the left," Ethan stated.

"What was?" Abbey asked, intrigued.

"His eyes, he looked up and to his left. That's remembering. If it was a statement of judgement he'd have looked at the result of the actions. At Susan."

"Got a temper too," Abbey added.

"Well, there's the pot calling the kettle names," Jameson said in a lighter manner, "which he calmed quickly. You questioned his work ethic, Swift. How did you expect him to react?"

"Expectation clouds observation," Ethan said. "It's not whether you'd expect him to react, it's that he did."

"And that he looks around," Jameson stated deprecatingly.

"Could be something and nothing," Ethan agreed. "Maybe he saw someone, something, maybe he feels he could've done more to help her, could be a self-criticism."

"I don't have a temper, I just don't tolerate stupidity. Which you two should take as a compliment," Abbey butted in with a mischievous grin.

Jameson rolled his eyes. "That mouth of yours is going to get you in trouble one day."

"Not with my two strong men around me," she said, linking arms with both of them and walking the length of the ward.

"Think you're equally capable of upsetting the grieving mother?" Ethan asked openly.

"Oh, more than," Abbey said with a touch of pride. "Lunch first though."

"Of course, can't go insulting people on an empty stomach."

"Wouldn't be right," Jameson agreed.

Lunch had consisted of a drive-through at McDonald's, much to Ethan's displeasure. Apparently it had always been Jameson's treat for the younger Swift when a successful day had been achieved or a case seen to conclusion. The idea that this be somewhat condescending and parental had been received far more fondly than Ethan had intended with Abbey leaning dotingly into Jameson and sucking her thumb as he placed a protective arm around her. As Jameson's protestations intensified so the determination of his joking colleagues was compounded. Upon arrival at window number one, Abbey took great delight in asking the young south Londoner made good his expert opinion on the establishment's fine cuisine.

"Always had a soft spot for chicken nuggets," Abbey conversed, leaning across Jameson to speak directly to the attendant.

"Is it?" the young man replied.

"Is it what?" Ethan asked, bemused, to nobody in particular. "That doesn't even make any sense."

"Can't all be as eloquent as you," Abbey said politely, looking into the back seat, drawing a chuckle from Jameson. "You may have the education, Doc, but this is from the university of life," she continued straight-faced, sending Jameson into an all-out guffaw.

"And people wonder how I put up with her all these years," Jameson surmised.

"What do you want then?" Abbey interrupted.

"Surprise me," Ethan said, defeated.

"Well, that should see me through for at least another twenty minutes," Ethan said aloud.

"Are you still moaning?" Abbey said, cupping her hand over the speaker of her mobile phone. "Don't pretend like you didn't enjoy it."

Jameson's eyes flashed up in the rear-view mirror, smiling as Ethan raised his eyebrows in a *what can you do?* response.

"I saw that," Abbey said knowingly as she returned to her phone conversation.

Lunch, for what it was worth, had finished some thirty minutes ago, and for the last twenty Abbey had been on the phone having information relayed to her regarding one Danny Jemson. With the dialogue of data having to contest with the sounds of the competing traffic, in-car entertainment had had to be supplied by a solo game of 'I spy' in Ethan's case, and the soundless directive of the satnav stuck to the window for

Jameson. Having won another, and final round of 'I spy', Ethan turned his attention to the miniature screen in front of him which was now counting down to less than a mile from their predetermined destination. Quite how the immediate area could change from its severe landscape to residential property time and time again in London, or any major city, had always fascinated Ethan, and captivated him once more as that very thought was punctuated by the turning of two sharp corners into what was not thirty seconds ago an invisible estate. It was clear that the houses, and affluence, grew as you ventured further up what was a steep incline, away from the last of the retail outlets, and into the private, more cultivated element of urban society. No doubt halfway up was an official partition in the boroughs, or if not, a fabricated one, providing the upper echelon the comfort of distancing themselves. As Jameson slowed the vehicle, searching for a parking space, it was clear they would not be crossing that divide on this occasion.

Abbey exhaled slowly, enjoying the break from receiving the barrage of information. "Well, where to start," she said as both sets of eyes turned to Abbey, waiting be filled in. "As expected, the girls didn't like him from day one. Liked it even less that Susan was willing to slum it," she emphasised. "Apparently he was too keen, always coming up with elaborate stories, led by misguided knowledge, wanting to impress. If one of their friends was going to China, young Danny had been there already, for every crazy night out someone had experienced, he'd had a wilder one, that kind of thing. It was tiresome. But, they knew it would be short-lived, as Susan was always going to outgrow him. When the inevitable happened, well, that's when they saw another side to the ardent Danny Jemson. Needless to say he didn't take it well."

"So don't," Ethan interrupted.

"Don't what?"

"Say it."

"Say what?" Abbey asked, perplexed.

"That he didn't take it well. If it's needless to say it, don't."

Abbey looked to Jameson with a bemused look and a shake of the head, but received only another stifled chortle in return.

"Anyway..."

"I'm just trying to keep us focused," Ethan affirmed, keeping a straight face, motioning for Abbey to continue, this time drawing a smile as she held her hands up in surrender.

"Anyway," she said, taking control of the conversation once more, "he started turning up at the apartment at all hours, often drunk, quick to temper, demanding to be seen, then suddenly pleading for a second chance and crying on the doorstep. If they ignored him long enough, eventually he'd disappear. And this is all within the past six weeks or so."

"He ever hurt her?" Jameson asked.

"They claimed he threatened them, the two friends. He'd seen them in town and they'd had words, but they never gave it any credence. Other than that, a fist through a couple of glass panes at the apartment building on his way out after a late-night visit."

"But not her," Ethan stated, rather than asked.

"Nope. He was of the belief that it was all their fault. They were the ones keeping them apart."

"Wow, a real modern-day Romeo and Juliet," Ethan suggested lamely.

"Ah, fair Verona," Jameson added, looking out at the surrounding landscape.

"There is, of course, one similarity."

"Which is?" Abbey asked, begrudging the further interruption.

"Romeo's dead," Ethan replied dryly, "and Juliet may yet join him."

"Well, Romeo has been in and out of work since leaving school, from the menial to the mundane, never holding anything down for any period of time. Fired from his last place, excessive non-work-related computer use. Not that!" Abbey snapped, cutting Jameson off before he could get the question out. "Nonplussed over the event apparently, happily gave the middle finger and walked out. His boss felt that he believed he was owed a living, he just wasn't willing to work for one. As for the home life, well that brings us to this lovely little domicile," she said, gesturing to the house on the left as if showing the emergency exits on an aeroplane. "Single parent family. Dad died a drunk before Danny reached his teen years, but not soon enough that he didn't get to witness domestic abuse as an everyday way of life. Neighbours say they'd hear him and his mother rowing, but as a general rule they kept themselves to themselves."

"Chapter and verse," Jameson concluded.

"So are we ready to go and see Lady Montague?" Abbey asked.

Ethan gave an approving nod, impressed, as the three of them climbed out of the car and descended on their joint victim/suspect's home.

"Oh yeah," Abbey mouthed silently to Ethan, tapping at her temple.

The door was opened after the third rap of Jameson's knuckles on the protruding wooden panel of the door.

"Yes?" the woman said breathlessly at barely more than a whisper as she filled the opening with her face, anything but invitingly.

"Mrs Jemson, I'm Detective Pat Jameson. Might we come in and talk to you about your son?" he said, holding out his identification at the right height for her eyeline.

Having sufficiently scrutinised the proffered credentials,

Mrs Jemson opened the door and shuffled off to the comfort of her armchair in the living room, never lifting a foot from the floor. Accepting the gracious invite as it was intended, Jameson led the way, following Danny's mother into the front room, while Ethan closed the door behind them. Having not been asked to sit, the three of them stood surveying the clutter, filling the cramped floor space as Mrs Jemson eyed them dispiritedly. It was only then that they could all see the dead look in her eyes. She had been crying, a lot. The eyes were bloodshot, red raw from the outpouring of emotion. No pictures, Ethan noticed as he looked around. The torrent of tears and expression of emotion had had its confinements. The surrounding walls would have offered no sympathy, just the stark reality of impending solitude.

"You just gonna stand there?" she husked.

"Mrs Jemson, we'd like your permission to take a look around Danny's bedroom," Jameson explained.

She shrugged, looking around the room at everything and nothing, before settling on the remote control on the sideboard and heaving her ample frame forward to grab it before falling back into her seated position.

"Don't you want to know who did this to your son?" Abbey asked, bemused.

"Bring him back will it?"

"Mrs Jemson..." Ethan began.

"Do what you like, you will anyway," she said, cutting him off, "then get out and leave me be."

Ethan gave his discreet approval as they moved out of the room toward the staircase in search of Danny's room.

"Obviously had a good experience with us before," Jameson commented as they turned to climb the stairs with the sound of the television coming to life behind them.

"I know the mum's no looker," Abbey said, stopping Ethan

and Jameson in their ascent, "but what do you think that is?" she asked, tilting her head and moving toward the mirror. "A hand maybe," she said, holding up a palm in front of the mirror, studying the two crack lines emitting outwards from the centre of the glass and lifting a second hand as if she were to lean forward and apply pressure.

"Try putting a body between you and the mirror," Ethan reasoned, moving down a couple of steps for a more even-levelled view.

"That'd work," Abbey agreed as she imagined two shoulders impacting the mirror under forceful retreat.

"So we know where it may have started," Jameson agreed. "You want to see where we know it finished?"

"Tidy little soul wasn't he," Abbey said as she flicked on the second of her latex gloves and started to lift the numerous items of clothing off the floor and surrounding furniture, unsure of what she was even looking for.

"So no one's done a once-over yet?" Abbey asked.

"Pronounced and escorted. Looked for all the world like natural causes or an undetermined suicide until Lucy threw the spanner," Jameson replied.

"It's still only a presumption that it wasn't," Ethan reasoned demurely.

"Are you questioning our great pathologist?" Abbey asked wryly, as she blindly tried to reach the shelving atop Danny's wardrobe.

"Not the physical findings."

"Just the theory on the perp," Jameson concluded for him.

"Indeed, although I can't fault her reasoning."

Abbey simply shrugged as the base of the wardrobe creaked

to a full crack under the pressure of her tiptoeing to gain a visual on the shelf.

"Should it do that?" she asked to no response.

"Explain to me why would you go from the anonymity of the unknown, from the safety of targeting the sub-city of society that the rest of us like to imagine doesn't even exist, to a young man, who lives at home, raising instant suspicions and enquiries. It doesn't make sense."

"Maybe nobodies weren't providing that thrill anymore," Jameson supposed. "You've always described it as a progressive business."

"It is, but this isn't progression. Every scene so far has been an exhibition of his capabilities. A statement of superiority. Where's the proclamation here? It hardly screams *look at me* does it," Ethan considered.

"Shipman's scene was that there was no scene. So he's staying authentic to the original," Jameson concurred.

"No, if it's our guy then there has to be a reason for simply getting the job done," Ethan said logically.

"You have got to be shitting me!" Abbey exclaimed from the base of the wardrobe, drawing their attention immediately away from supposition back to the present reality.

"Out of the mouths of babes," Jameson said breezily.

Abbey knelt by the wardrobe, ripping at the boards that had struggled to cope with her light frame and tossing them on the floor beside her as she looked wide-eyed into the newly made recess.

"Fuck a duck," she said in a drawn-out fashion as she lifted a metal speculum from the recess, turning open-mouthed to her audience of two.

"That would be a reason," Ethan said serenely.

"Pat, I want a full forensics down here now," Abbey demanded. "Our latest victim just became our lead suspect."

CHAPTER THIRTY-THREE

Theodore Hewitt held his arms aloft to quieten the multitude of reporters awaiting confirmation of the news. He had risen through the ranks as quickly as his frame had expanded. To think that the deputy commissioner had once had to pass a fitness test of any sort now defied belief. Never too proud to flatter the senior administration or too righteous to tread upon his peers, 'Teddy Hewitt' now sat as commissioner elect just waiting for the old man to vacate the throne. 'Teddy' had been his idea to bring him closer to the city's constituents, a persona that when mixed with the overzealous grin that was wheeled out upon every triumph had been latched onto fondly by the city press. Here stood a man, who had succeeded alone, and failed, due only to the flaws of his subordinates. A self-promoting outlook that had carried him far, but had him perceived in a very different light from within the police force than from those reliant upon it.

"Gentleman, and ladies of course," Theodore began, flashing the renowned grin at a couple of female media correspondents who had made it to the front of the pack, "while I appreciate the rumour mill has an expected amount of output, as does any business," a ripple of half-hearted laughter worked its way around the crowd until Teddy was satisfied everyone had partaken, "I will have to cut production off at source on this one as I am pleased to confirm that we have indeed achieved a most agreeable resolution in the recent copycat killings investigation," he continued, concluding each statement with a return of the fervent beam of self-satisfaction. "While a young woman continues her fight for survival, her family, and indeed the woman herself can exult in the knowledge her fight is not in vain. For it was due to her courage and defiance in the face of personal peril that allowed our fine force to isolate and converge on Mr Danny Jemson. The only regrettable consequence of this, is that as has proved to be the case all too often, when reality engulfs these degenerates of society, they refuse to stand accountable for their actions. I can also therefore confirm that Mr Jemson was found to have taken his own life upon our team's arrival at his place of residence. And while it is our preferred practice to see justice delivered as it is meant to be, the good people of our capital can once again feel safe in the knowledge that its public servants have undeniably, served them admirably."

As the deputy commissioner let the silence sit briefly, the clamour of questions roared forward as the collection before him erupted into activity, desperate to be given the nod of approval and accompanying respect to have their individual questions heard.

"Teddy, what support do you give to the notion that Danny Jemson was a victim also?" a solitary voice called forward as Theodore Hewitt's sizeable pointer brought the crowd to a hush.

"A victim?" the deputy commissioner said, chewing at his lower lip, pondering the idea incredulously as he surveyed the gathering. "I have no doubt he was, but he was a victim to nothing more than the weight of his own guilt and fear of our equitable repercussions."

Superintendent Meadows turned away from his window view of the impromptu press conference below, shaking his head in disbelief as he turned his attention to Ethan and Abbey sat expectantly in front of him.

"The fact that that is a complete fabrication of events doesn't come into it then?" Ethan asked.

"There's the truth, and there's the deputy commissioner's truth," Meadows reasoned.

"And Teddy's bullshit," Abbey added.

"The case remains open, we continue without disruption, and the public get peace of mind."

"And when it's proven that success was heralded more than a touch early?" Ethan posed.

"Ain't a top invented Theodore couldn't spin," Meadows responded resignedly. "What does our truth tell us?" he asked, falling into the seat behind his desk.

"Vaginal fluid and blood on the speculum matches our lady of the night," Abbey began. "Puts him at the scene at least. Nothing else within the bedroom to tie in to any of the other copies. No medicinal supplies or implements to administer the missing diamorphine. So unless he managed to clear up after his successful suicide..." she said sarcastically with a bemused shake of her head.

"Anything else?" Meadows asked sternly.

Abbey flicked pages over on an imaginary notebook, scanning the pages for information. "Yep, here it is, er, SOCO guys said he lived in a shithole."

"Which just on its own is enough to indicate he isn't the source. You remember my lecture you walked in on, Tony? The prevention of terrorist cells. Same applies. You've got the recruitment and the foot soldiers. Danny Jemson..."

"Foot soldier," Meadows finished for him.

"And a court-martialled one at that. The cause might not be as inspirational, but this is a recruitment and fulfilment campaign. Of that I'm sure."

"Which leaves us where?"

"Looking for a tree in the middle of a fucking forest," Abbey offered.

Ethan smiled softly at his venting partner. "With two possible avenues we can affect."

"So where does the initial conscription take place?" Meadows asked. "Trust has to be built up. That takes time, persuasion and coercion."

"Anonymous crazy seeks angry youths of the world. Catchy. Only the interweb can cater to such poignant personal ads as that," Abbey suggested.

"Have we checked Danny's PC?" Meadows asked.

"They turned it on, but it was passworded, would've left it at that. It'll have been collected though, and we can take a closer look once it's on site."

CHAPTER THIRTY-FOUR

Ethan and Abbey walked among the crowd enjoying the light entertainment provided by the street performers at either end of the Covent Garden square. A hubbub of conversation and relaxed merriment as people met up after the working day, mixing synonymously with the tourists enjoying the fascination of seeing the city change from its daytime functionality to provide residents and visitors alike with a wealth of nightly activities to take pleasure in.

"How do you think he does it?" Abbey asked, taking in the atmosphere as much as anyone else as she spiked a chip drenched in vinegar from its newspaper wrapping.

"Does what?" Ethan replied through a mouthful of fried potato.

"Lovely. When this is all over with, how about you take me out for a real dinner?" Abbey asked, raising her eyebrows as she spiked another chip, an uneasy silence suddenly apparent as Ethan was stuck between a half smile and swallowing hard.

"How do you think he gets their trust, persuades them to act on his say-so?" Abbey added hurriedly, focusing intently on the ever-moistening wrapping.

"I'd imagine they're the type who don't need much persuasion," Ethan reasoned as they continued to stroll aimlessly around the square, families and couples rushing to finish their meals or last minute of allotted shopping time before heading to the surrounding theatres to complete their day out in the big smoke. "Better question would be how they gain his trust."

"They're the ones who do his 'work'," Abbey said, adding air quotes. "Surely they are more trusting of him?"

"Its twofold really, anonymity is paramount, so we have to presume he remains faceless, killing the trail before it's even in place. Secondly, the execution has to be clinical, precision is as important, if not more so, than the act itself. That is why he needs to trust them. To ensure their negligence doesn't reflect badly on his overall vision."

"How'd you do that? Danny Jemson strike you as somebody meticulous in nature?" Abbey said with a heavy sigh.

"No, he doesn't," Ethan answered softly, almost to himself, his walk slowing and dropping behind Abbey's stride as he reviewed the crime scene in his mind.

"It's like you said," Ethan stated, the vigour returning to his voice as Abbey looked back over her shoulder, slowing her own gait. "Angry youths of the world. That's why the trust isn't an issue. They're online, out in the world, whatever, just looking for a reason to act out. But they're not just given a reason, a cause, they are provided with a blueprint, a step-by-step guide, where tools, venue, date and time are all provided for them. All they have to do is join the dots. He'd still be reliant on emotions being tempered, but if they run, he's a ghost, an annoyance maybe, but nothing more. If they are frenzied, that would probably be his bigger fear, but with victims selected randomly and probably unknown before the act itself, how can emotion play a factor?"

"So we understand him better. How the twisted little game may play out. But you just summed it up, Doc. He's a ghost."

CHAPTER THIRTY-FIVE

"Good morning, Janice," Ethan said to the young woman on reception for the morning shift of the open all hours glorified port of call for lost property. "Any messages? And I didn't get my wake-up call again."

Janice returned only a bleak, half-hearted smile rather than the usual full beam of being given the recognition that she even be there as a functioning part of the Met's operation. She was all too aware that the majority saw her only as window dressing for the simple and menial tasks of a desk jockey. Ethan had been different though. No inflated ego or sense of self-importance, he had been impressed that she found the time to earn as well as put herself through college in order to serve the law by a different means. Those that hadn't given her the respect she deserved would look at her very differently when it came to placing their methods and results under her scrutiny. And Ethan had promised her that her time would come.

"Mr Meadows would like to see you straight away. Ms Swift is already with him, Mr Marshall," she said softly.

"No problem, and it's Ethan. I can't be old enough to be called a mister by someone in their twenties, surely."

The smile returned as Janice nodded, acknowledging the instruction.

"Morning Tony, Ms Swift," Ethan said, sliding himself into the chair next to Abbey.

"You ask Janice for your messages?" Meadows said dryly.

"That predictable, huh."

"How'd she react?"

"Yeah, not so funny today apparently."

"Or any day," Abbey countered, drawing a rueful shake of the head from Ethan.

"That's because you have one!"

"Here? From who?" Ethan asked, frowning.

"For the attention of Mr Ethan Marshall," Meadows began, handing over a laser-jet sheet of A4 paper, "hot off the presses."

FAO Mr Ethan Marshall

Dearest Ethan,

I find the lack of column inches rather unamusing. I know it isn't the media's fault. The police chief likes to keep these things quiet. Who will be next? Oh so many to choose from, to imitate. I guess to you it seems senseless, but I simply cannot help myself. Good luck hunting.

P.S. I think it is time I had a better name for me, for my work. I would not suggest insulting your intelligence by providing examples, I'll leave it in your capable hands.

"Came through the contacts page on the website. Thanking the Met. You believe that?" Meadows said, breaking the silence as Ethan took in the words before him again.

"How'd they get my name? It's not been published in the press. Even if they are aware of my involvement."

"Money talks," Abbey said. "Who's to say some halfwit didn't think they were earning themselves a buck by talking to a reporter."

"This seems more personal than that."

"It mean anything to you?" Meadows asked.

"It stays true to the trend. It's a copycat, only this time a literary one. Dennis Rader, BTK, killed ten victims in the state of Kansas. Gave himself the moniker, short for bind, torture, kill. Sent letters and poems to local police and then newspapers in search of greater coverage for his works. 'Good luck hunting' became the infamous message as he continued to elude capture."

"So why make contact?"

"Because he can," Abbey said dejectedly. "He's flaunting his anonymity."

"In all probability," Ethan agreed. "Alternatively, if it is more than just a name he has paid for he may see my introduction, my involvement, as a personal challenge to his intelligence."

"Either way, there is no record of receipt or verification from the initial source that we can trace backwards to find where the message originated from," Meadows explained, "the beauty of the internet."

"A haven for the faceless," Abbey added.

Ethan rubbed his hands across his face. "The question of why make contact is still relevant," he said, bridging his fingers.

"You have a theory?" Abbey posed inquisitively.

"I do."

"Care to share?" Meadows supplicated.

"Not just yet," Ethan replied, drumming his steepled fingers.

Abbey looked at Meadows beseechingly, receiving only a barely noticeable shake of the head in return.

Ethan sat tapping his fingers, every so often pausing to rest them on his upper lip while Meadows turned his focus to the mountain of papers on his desk, scribbling approval and rejection in equal quantity while Abbey sat exasperated, looking between the two men, wondering when the meeting had officially ended.

"Well then..." she said aloud to no response as she motioned to leave the room.

A rap on the door was followed by the large frame of PC Johnson casting a shadow across the room and swiftly entering, nearly hitting Abbey up the side of the head, resulting in a none too welcoming glare at her subordinate.

"Woah, sorry, boss lady, I mean, ma'am."

"Do you never wait for permission to enter, Johnson?" Meadows asked without lifting his head.

"Sorry, sir, just that other confession, the young lad claiming responsibility. Well, he's out front, saying something about a letter he shouldn't have sent."

Ben Davies sat alone in the interview room trying to calm his breathing, glancing around at his cold surroundings, now understanding why so many people were so easily broken on television shows when placed in such an environment. He'd seen it countless times. The tough, couldn't be shaken wrongdoer, reduced to a shell of their persona in just minutes. The sanitised feel of the room had the ability to make him feel as if he were the only dirty item in attendance, and a clear conscience would provide the equivalent feeling of a hot shower cleansing the body after a tough workout, or ridding himself of the dust and dirt accumulated when cleaning out his mother's garage. Ben had chosen to come alone, to take responsibility and face up to what he had done. What had he done? He wasn't sure that he had actually committed a crime. But if that were the case, why did he have that bottomless feeling in his stomach, and the weight of his mother's disappointment on his slight shoulders.

Ethan and Abbey made their way down to the interview room, pausing outside, wondering what to expect on the other side.

"The crazies don't usually come back after being dismissed so easily," Ethan said, to himself as much as to Abbey.

"Not until the next big case anyway," she replied with a grin. "So are we thinking this is on the up and up?"

Ethan blew out his cheeks, pressing down slowly and deliberately on the door's handle. "Maybe we have our first foot soldier. Our first live one anyway."

Abbey and Ethan had been sat across from the young man for over fifteen minutes, still trying to begin the interview in earnest after several false starts. Ben sat sobbing, his words trying to form, but getting lost in his ever-increasing hyperventilation and free-flowing mucus mixing with the tears that continued to dispense until they both met the barrier of spittle now formed on his top lip.

"You've got to talk to us, Ben," Abbey said soothingly. "Let us know what happened. How it happened."

Ben nodded sheepishly as he stuttered through another breath, wiping his sleeve across the bottom half of his face.

"I just wanted to protect my mum," he managed, "and now I've just made everything worse. If he doesn't hurt her, then he will instead."

"If who doesn't who will?" Ethan asked softly. "Who are you afraid of, Ben?"

"I don't even know him," Ben bawled.

"Hey, hey, slow down. You want to help, Ben, I can see that. Hell, you wouldn't be here if you didn't," Abbey offered, "but you've got to walk us through this, baby steps, you understand?"

Another sheepish acknowledgment accompanied a stammering intake of breath.

"You want a drink, or something to eat maybe?" Ethan asked.

Ben shook his head, not looking at Ethan but seeking comfort in Abbey, who reached out a hand, placing it on top of his, encouraging him to continue.

"I just wanted him gone. My stepfather, sorry," Ben quickly elaborated, seeing Abbey's imploring look.

"No need to be sorry, honey, you're doing great."

"Thanks," Ben said with his first genuine smile since he had arrived.

"You're not in any trouble here, Ben."

"He said... he said, if I did something for him, then he'd help me with my problem, that he'd get rid of my dad, my stepdad," he corrected himself, "but then when I couldn't do it, he said I had to send the email. And if I didn't, then a little domestic violence would be the least of my worries."

Ethan nodded at Abbey to proceed as Ben took a tighter grip on her hand.

"What did he ask you to do, Ben?"

"*Strangers on a Train*. But I didn't want to hurt anyone, I..."

"He asked you to kill somebody?" Ethan asked in astonishment, wondering how the child before him was expected to do such a thing. However these followers were recruited, the employer had got this one very wrong. "How, who?"

Abbey shot Ethan a look of derision to stop him in his tracks.

"Some old guy," Ben said, looking at Ethan for the first time. "He said he'd done bad things, to kids, you know. But when I saw him, he just looked like an old man."

"You went there?" Abbey coaxed.

"Uh-huh," Ben mumbled. "But I couldn't do anything. I didn't want to do anything," he said hastily before the inevitable question could be asked. "And then when he saw me, I ran."

"Where was this, Ben?"

Ben shoved his hand in his coat pocket, pulling out two crumpled sheets of paper that had been stapled together, and throwing them on the table, wanting rid of them as hurriedly as he could manage from his bare hands. Two pages of printed notation were visible even on the infolded sheets, while a neatly handwritten address stared up at the three room attendees.

Ethan took a tissue from his own pocket and slowly lifted the sheets in thumb and forefinger for a closer inspection, shaking them loose as he took in the printed instruction.

"And this was to be followed?" Ethan asked.

Ben nodded solemnly, bouncing his leg nervously.

"To the letter. He made it quite clear."

"And the tools, the equipment?"

"It was all left in a bin, outside the underground. I waited for it to be clear and just grabbed it before anyone could see," Ben explained through shallow breaths.

"And after you ran?" Abbey asked.

"I dumped it in the bin outside Seven Sisters station. I should've kept that too, shouldn't I?" Ben replied, his shoulders slumping.

"Not to worry, Ben," Ethan offered. "That's what people like Detective Swift are good at finding. What they really need your help on is how you met this man. The one who wanted you to do this for him."

"I never met him," Ben said, shaking his head, looking from Ethan to Abbey and back again. "And I don't want to!"

"So how..." Ethan probed in a confused manner, desperate for their theory to be validated.

"Through the site," Ben confirmed.

CHAPTER THIRTY-SIX

"Must be nice to have at least part of your profile proved correct," Abbey said, suppressing a smile.

"Part of!" Ethan said incredulously, as they made their way to the newly formed incident room. "You're still not giving me the age?"

"Can't," Abbey said with a shake of the head. "It's all about the evidence, Ethan. And I've nothing confirming anything other than known perpetrators are in their early twenties. Sorry," she concluded, no longer trying to hide her grin.

"And almost one who was barely halfway through his teens. That has to have been a mistake. No way would our man have entrusted his great vision onto a child. He wants to manipulate, not babysit," Ethan concluded.

"Shall we?" she offered, pushing the door open for Ethan.

The newly furnished room was similar to that of the IT room at the college, and to that at Ethan's own senior school. Monitors and processors may look sleeker, take up less space, and be infinitely quicker than yesteryear, but there really was only so many ways a computer room could look. Five monitors were in full operation, individually manned, all logged on to the same website, the users typing away while the workstation whirred below. Two empty chairs sat at the far end of the horseshoe, facing blacked-out screens. Adam Derry stood over the shoulder of one of the officers, scanning the text and taking in the data readings at the foot of the screen.

"And switch," he said, tapping the shoulder of the user.

Adam had come into the force more by accident than design. Brought in as a contactor in order to manage a network installation, he happened to be on hand when numerous security measures needed to be bypassed on a recently seized consignment of laptops which had been recovered during the process of breaking a local paedophile ring. The excitement of such productive IT work, coupled with the Met's own enthusiasm to recruit him on a permanent basis made the decision a simple one. Four years on, and he still got the buzz of being brought onto a case. Busying himself and those around him, his appetite was infectious.

"Hey, Abbey," Adam said, pulling himself away from his virtual surroundings.

"Hey yourself. This is Ethan Marshall. Ethan, this is geeky Adam."

"Hi, Ethan," he said, shaking his hand. "So you're the guy who knows how people work."

"And you all this," Ethan said, gesturing to the room.

"Indeed. A whole lot easier if you ask me. Too many variables with people. Computers, they do what they're asked to do. And let you know what they've already done."

"So what do we have here?" Ethan asked.

"Well," Adam began, pointing to each of the officers in turn, "here we have Dan, Dave, Doug, Donald and Derek..."

"You're shitting me," Abbey interrupted.

"I shit you not. Though they are of course the names of the machines only. The *people*, I believe you call them?" he said looking to Ethan for approval, "I've no idea. Purely for decoration. They're incidental."

Ethan smiled at his new host, liking him immediately, while Abbey could only shake her head.

"And?" She gestured for him to explain.

"Five users, running several pseudonyms. None for an elongated period of time. Nothing greater than a seventy-minute period. Then switch the pseudonym and repeat. It's a fishing expedition."

"Seventy minutes?" Ethan asked.

"Yep, contrary to the image that those skulking the internet are on there twenty-four seven, the average time for a regular user is seventy minutes. We stay on for too long then we may attract the attention of those we're trying to lure. You don't want to scare the fish unless you have to."

Adam turned and walked to the central console filling the majority of the horseshoe and tapped the nearest of the three monitors with some affection.

"All that data then feeds through to *Beth* here. If there's a pattern to be found, keywords, extended usage, lurking, she'll track it. She's a mechanical Swift, ruthless," Adam concluded, chuckling.

"And those two?" Ethan asked, casting an eye over the two vacant chairs.

"They're the interesting ones," Adam replied with intrigue. "Mr Davies will be coming in with his computer later today and that'll give us an insight into the workings and activity of the last few months. The other will be from Mr Jemson. Unfortunately we don't have the luxury of him walking us through his passwords and security measures. But I'll find a spare ten minutes from somewhere," Adam said mischievously.

"Well, we'll leave you and *Beth* to it shall we," Abbey said. "Be sure to let us know once you've worked your ten minutes of magic, wouldn't want to interrupt," she said with an impish longing.

"Abbey... no need for jealousy. There's plenty of room for both you and *Beth*. Open relationships are all the rage."

"Well, I've known a few who've had relationships with their hard drive," Abbey replied, coughing, "all it got them was bad eyesight and a sore wrist!"

CHAPTER THIRTY-SEVEN

"What must've been going through his mind when he was walking from the station to here? That's a lot of thinking time," Ethan considered as they made their way up the path to the old man's front door.

"He looked like he was carrying the weight of the world when he spoke to us. Must've been tenfold at the time. You ready?" Abbey asked as she rapped on the front door. "Always such nice surroundings."

The wheezing cough could be heard even before the old man shuffled into the entrance hall, dragging his air supply behind him. Tiny shuffled footsteps brought the man ever closer to the front door, his feet struggling to break contact with the worn carpet, eyeing them curiously through the glass pane and studying the mottled figures suspiciously.

"What you want?" the old man asked hoarsely as he pried open the door until the chain caught.

"Good afternoon, sir, I'm DI Swift, and this is Mr Marshall. Could you spare us some of your time? It's about an incident you had here..."

"What incident?" the man cut in. "I never reported any incident."

"That may be so, but the young man..."

"Young hooligan," the man cut in again, breaking into a hacking cough.

"Sir, if we could just come in," Ethan asked softly, receiving no more than a grunt of recognition before the door closed, and reopened once more without the safety-catch restriction.

"Tea's in the cupboard, milk's in the fridge. Might as well make yourself useful while you're here," he said breathlessly, shuffling off to the warmth of the sitting room.

"Shotgun," Abbey whispered, "mine's white with one. Thanks ta."

"So you caught the kid," the old man said matter of factly as he took the mug from Ethan.

"Actually, sir, he came to us," Abbey informed him.

"Harry, call me Harry."

"Any idea why he was here, Harry?" Ethan asked.

"Just kids playing around I guess. I figured he had his mates round the corner. You remember knock down ginger?" Harry asked, looking at Abbey.

"I do," Abbey replied, reddening slightly.

"Must've played it dozens of times when I was a youngster. Turns out it's not so much fun on the other side of the door," he explained, breaking into another bout of uncontrollable dry coughing.

"Sounds like you've got razors in your throat," Ethan offered.

"And feels like it too, son. Let me tell you this. You ever get to this stage," he said, gesturing to his general state and air-supply apparatus, "well, just don't let it get to this stage. Now surely you have greater concerns in this grand city of ours than an old man being bothered."

"Well," Abbey began tentatively, "we don't think it was a kids being kids kind of problem. In fact, we know it wasn't."

"You've seen the copycat news stories?" Ethan asked.

"Of course," Harry confirmed, looking from Ethan to Abbey and waiting for the silence to be filled. "You think I was a target! He was just a kid."

"I'm afraid so," Ethan said solemnly. "It would appear that they, these young adults, are recruited."

"Recruited by who exactly?"

"And therein lies the rub," Ethan replied.

"We don't know," Abbey said. "Not yet. Which is why we need your help. Can you think of anyone, any reason why you may be singled out?"

"Maybe they knew I wanted out! Take a look around, love. I can't breathe without help. I'm in constant pain."

"This wouldn't be a mercy killing. Every one of the victims suffered. There's no reason to think you'd be treated with any leniency," Ethan explained.

"Look at me. Whatever happened, it would've been an act of clemency. All my friends have passed away. I've been a widower for the last eight years. The only time I get visitors are to make sure I've still got a pulse. And they're half the problem! It's not how I envisaged seeing out my days."

"In what way?" Ethan asked.

"In what way what?" Harry replied, confused, wincing as he tried to swallow.

"In what way are they a problem? Your medical support."

"By not letting things be. I've been this close," Harry detailed, holding his fingers just millimetres apart, "this close to passing over, making the transition, dying. Whatever label you want to put on it. And twice the meddlesome do-gooders have pulled me back from the brink. Back to this. And they wonder why I'm not doing a dance of gratitude."

Harry broke out into another fit of coughing, weary from the extended conversation, his body searching for rest, looking even smaller in his chair than when they had first arrived. Abbey nodded silently to Ethan as Harry's eyes closed and then slowly refocused on his guests as he fought against the ensuing slumber.

"Thanks, Harry," Abbey said fondly, placing her hand on his as she made her way past. A smatter of recognition was the last sound they heard as Harry drifted off to less painful climes, allowing them to make their way back out of the property and onto the streets.

"Anything useful?" Abbey asked, wrapping her coat tightly round her as the wind picked up once more, offering a further chill to the returning inclement weather.

"Well, I think I know who we're looking at. Or what they do at the very least. If you think that's useful," Ethan said with a shrug and a smile as he walked ahead to get back into the car.

"Pray tell."

"You already know," Ethan said, shoving his hands in his pockets and making his way down the path, leaving Abbey looking confused on the front step.

CHAPTER THIRTY-EIGHT

"So how do you know?" Abbey asked as they made their way through the station's winding corridors to meet with Adam and see just what secrets *Beth* had extracted from the newly installed computer terminals.

"I don't know. To know would suggest proof. But I do know," Ethan said with a mischievous grin.

"Sadly, a lot of people are known to have done something. That's why there's the burden of proof."

"A ridiculous requirement!" Ethan said. "The old man was selected because he didn't deserve to live," he continued.

"What?"

"Not my thoughts," Ethan said defensively. "To say our puppeteer has a mild case of NPD and egocentrism is to call Santa Claus fat and jolly. These are the very traits that define him. Not simply describe him."

"NPD?" Abbey enquired, slowing their pace as she took in the information.

"Narcissistic Personality Disorder. These are people who seek perfection, happy to take advantage and manipulate others."

"Sounds like every serial killer ever profiled," Abbey said resignedly.

"Perhaps. They also take to criticism with spontaneous anger, believing themselves to be beyond reproach. That sound more familiar?"

"It's a little tenuous don't you think?"

"The old man was ungrateful each time he was resuscitated. I know from my own experiences with my father, the carers, as good as they are, when it comes to actual medical attention they are strictly hands off. Protocol states that they call for paramedics. Maybe it wasn't on both occasions, but on the latest occurrence, I'll bet a twenty to your pound I can name the paramedic who resuscitated him."

"If you were a betting man," Abbey teased.

"Hey, PC Adam. You see what I did there?" Abbey said, announcing her entrance into the IT room.

"Oh, because I work with computers, and I'm employed by the police force," Adam replied sardonically. "Very witty."

The five operators offered no acknowledgement or realisation that new personnel had appeared within their actual world, still deeply lost in their virtual equivalent. Sat at each of the five terminals they'd been designated, key-tapping continuously, the click-clacking the only sound over and above the hum of the server equipment, working tirelessly to find something of relevance.

"I thought so," Abbey confirmed, grinning. "So what have you got for us, geeky?"

"In a nutshell, I know your perp's handle," Adam offered resignedly.

"That's not good news?" Ethan asked.

"Yes and no. Good in that we can track his usage. Bad in

that he is recorded as logging on from all over the world. So any help in locating him or putting a face to the user is currently impossible. He knows his stuff."

"Don't they always," Abbey stated.

Adam walked over to one of the two machines that had been added at the end of the horseshoe.

"Can offer you very little from young Benjamin," he stated, placing his hand on top of the monitor in front of him. "He's a scared young man, wanting to help his mum and be rid of his stepfather. Social media, while minimal in terms of friends and activity, simply supports his unhappiness. The few friends he does have are supportive as much as anyone can be through Facebook. Internet history shows searches for divorce, restraining orders, why people stay in abusive relationships. He was trying to understand as well as finding ways out. Nothing to suggest he wanted to hurt anyone though, until very recently when he stumbled upon our beloved forum."

"So something must have happened at home. There will have been a trigger of some kind," Ethan surmised.

"You'd have to think so."

"Initially he just watched, lurking, reading what others had to say. With so much chatter, and so many different people active it probably gave him confidence to join in."

"Safety in numbers I guess," Abbey said.

"And they'd have known he was there too. A list of those logged on is readily available at the bottom of the forum. Anyone with an active interest in monitoring users will have seen him on there for weeks before he eventually spoke. Even when he joined in, he gave nothing but the impression, and an accurate one at that, that he was simply a vulnerable adolescent looking for help. Desperate for it. So desperate that he jumped at the first offer of a resolution that was put forward."

"And now he's even more scared of what might happen for coming to his senses," Ethan offered.

"Absolutely. Now Mr Jemson was very different, mind." Adam began turning his attention to the set-up opposite.

"Shocker. More the manipulative callous type than vulnerable. Wouldn't you say, Doc?" Abbey offered.

"Also on social media but on a grander scale. Self-promotion came easily to him. Web searches are more than a little disturbing. Researched how to kill, disposing of bodies, famous serials. Has a liking for pornography, but not your standard stuff. He has an extensive library of torture and submission porn. And real or not, we've yet to prove, but in the six months leading up to your murders, he downloaded two videos I can only label as snuff films."

"Where are these men when you're really looking for one though?" Abbey asked. "I'm just a lonely girl looking to spend some quality time with someone."

"Can't imagine he held a job down for too long either, considering the hours he has as an online gamer," Adam continued.

"And the forum?" Ethan prompted.

"A busy boy. Very active. Liked to rile others up whenever he could. But even in his case, it wasn't until Tutor – that's your man – came on, that he really pushed on from aspiring to, to executing."

"Pertinent choice of word, Adam," Ethan countered. "Anything else?"

"Nothing of note," Adam concluded, offering his hand before Ethan and Abbey started to take their leave.

"For what it's worth his moniker was Clown," Adam added without turning round.

"Clown, like the whole thing's a fucking joke. Arsehole!" Abbey said aloud to no one in particular.

"That may hold more relevance than you think," Ethan said contentedly.

"You want me to do what?" Meadows asked. "And our reason for doing this? You do remember we need a reason, Ethan. There's no chance I'll get a warrant to arrest a man on supposition and your say-so."

Ethan sat quietly, with Abbey next to him as he let the superintendent vent his bewilderment.

"I'm not saying I don't trust you, Ethan," Meadows continued, not letting the silence settle.

"And why wouldn't you?" Ethan said with a smile.

"I'm just saying we need more."

"You won't need it," Ethan said, shaking his head. "He'll want to come in."

"Why would he want to come in?" Abbey asked.

"For exactly the reasons Tony states. We have nothing on him, and he'll revel in that. And I don't want him arrested, I want him invited in for a chat. And even that is reliant on checking one other bit of information first."

"Tread very carefully, Ethan," Meadows stated forcefully.

"Is that a yes?" Abbey asked excitedly. "I bet the cocky sod will be thrilled to see me again. Can I do the invite, Ethan... please?" she pleaded.

"Out," Meadows ordered, pointing at the door.

"Maybe," Ethan replied. "We've got one more thing to check before we do anything. And then we've a quick errand to run as well."

CHAPTER THIRTY-NINE

Abbey sat behind the wheel as Ethan clicked his seatbelt into place.

"So what's your errand?"

"Our errand," Ethan offered. "I want to see how Ben and his mum are doing."

"I didn't have you down as care in the community, Ethan. Not en route to catching a killer anyway."

"I like to take the road less travelled, so maybe I am."

"Okay," Abbey said slowly, turning the key and pulling out of the car park.

The traffic had been surprisingly light and it turned out that the detour hadn't proved as much of a hindrance as Abbey had envisaged. Abbey had managed to pull up kerbside looking out of her window at the peaceful setting.

"Nightmare in suburbia, eh?"

"Who knows what goes on behind the white picket fence," Ethan agreed.

As they walked up the garden path they saw the curtain

twitch in the front window, and by the time they reached the front door the chain could already be heard unlatching. The door opened before a knock was necessary and Benjamin stood before them.

"Hey, Ben," Abbey said jovially. "How are you doing? Is your mum in?"

"Uh-huh," he said sheepishly.

"Who is it?" a voice shouted from within.

All of a sudden a tall, well-built man in his mid-forties came out of the doorway, presumably leading to the front room, his face dropping in disgust as he saw his unwanted visitors.

"What the fuck d'you want?" he moaned. "This about this little fuck-up? Go on, get back inside," he continued, shoving Ben away from the door.

"Good afternoon, sir, may we come in briefly?" Ethan asked.

"Like a no is gonna keep you out, right?" the man said, retreating back to the lounge.

"Not working today, sir?" Abbey asked as they followed him in, closing the door behind them.

The lounge was like a million other front rooms across the country. Neat enough but best described as lived in. It would shortly reach the point where it demanded cleaning, but it wasn't at the point of embarrassment should unexpected guests turn up on your doorstep. The television was on. The mindless numb of daytime TV filling the void of the day.

"In between jobs," he said with a shrug, falling into the armchair opposite the screen.

Mrs Davies sat meekly in the armchair askew from the TV. Ethan nodded to Abbey as he smiled reassuringly at Ben.

"Mrs Davies, I'm Ethan Marshall, this is DI Swift. We'd like to talk to you about your son if that's okay?"

Mrs Davies adjusted herself uncomfortably in the chair, pulling her sleeves down both forearms as they rode up slightly, showing bruising on both wrists, looking up at her partner the whole time.

"Or maybe you'd like to talk to Miss Swift while your husband makes us all a cup of tea?" Ethan proposed as he retrieved his mobile phone from his pocket, reading the newly arrived message.

"We're not married," she said timidly.

"That'll be right," the man offered, not moving. "You want a cup of tea, you can get your own at a café."

"Why don't I just make it for us then. I'm sure I can find the kettle," Ethan suggested, looking to make his way out of the room. "I'm sure I won't need to do a full walk around."

"Damn right you won't," the man stated, springing to his feet and putting his hand up and into Ethan's chest.

"Sir, that right there is an assault on an officer," Abbey said quickly.

"You are fucking kidding me," he replied.

"No need for that, Swift. Something and nothing, right?" Ethan asked the man, still stood awkwardly holding his hand up, unsure what to do next.

"All we're doing is going to the kitchen to put the kettle on."

"Fine," the man grumbled.

"Why'd you want me out the room anyway," the man asked as he begrudgingly filled the kettle at the faucet and clicked it on at its base.

"We just came round to tell her she need not worry about her boy. He won't be facing any trouble from us. In fact, he didn't really do anything wrong."

"Nothing wrong," the man tutted, "other than bring the bizzies round here you mean."

"Seems to me like you warranted a visit," Ethan replied.

"Me? You got fuck all on me, mate."

"I'm not your mate," Ethan countered. "How long you been out of work?"

"A year, eighteen months. Times are tough." The man sniggered.

"But not for you," Ethan offered matter of factly. "In fact, I'd imagine that's about the same time you got with Mrs Davies."

"What do you know about that?" the man asked, frowning.

"I read people well. We all have a skill set. Similar to yours for charming and then intimidating vulnerable and susceptible women."

"And you think I care what you think of me? Ain't a crime to have some bizzies dislike me."

"Nope, it's not. But it might be if we take a closer look at those bruises on Mrs Davies's wrists. Or ask her where else she may have had injuries recently. Hospital records will answer some of that though."

"What can I say, she's accident prone."

"They so often are," Ethan surmised, noticing that the kettle had switched itself off, having reached its own boiling point.

"And not a lot you, or your rozzer buddies can do about it," the man bragged, pointing a finger.

Ethan stepped forward quickly, grasping the finger and bending it back, watching as the smug look on the man's face turned to a grimace.

"The thing is," Ethan said in a whisper, "I'm not a rozzer or a bizzie, or any other term you want to use. I'm a consultant, and with that, a member of the public. So I could, if provoked, defend myself from any aggressive affront I feel warranted it."

The man gritted his teeth and moved to grab Ethan, but instead ended up dropping to his knee with a stifled yelp, eyes starting to stream, as Ethan applied more pressure to his index finger, bending it back to what at least felt like its snapping point.

"Now," Ethan continued, "I'm not one to break up a happy home. So you have two options, you either improve as a husband... sorry, partner. Or, you can make your excuses, or don't, and leave, letting this home become a happy one."

"Like you get to make that decision," the man managed through gritted teeth.

"Your decision entirely," Ethan proposed, "but if you do stay, then you can expect some regular visits from your local fine upstanding constabulary, just to ensure that you are the man they need you to be."

Ethan let go of the man's finger who visibly sized up Ethan, debating what to do next.

"Best leave the tea, they'll be almost done in the other room," Ethan concluded, taking his leave and returning to the front room.

Ethan entered to see both Mrs Davies and Ben smiling at Abbey.

"Thank you," Mrs Davies mouthed, no words coming out.

"We all done then?" Ethan asked.

"We are," Abbey said with a smile of her own, turning to an inquisitive look at Ethan as Mrs Davies's partner followed him in cradling his finger.

"No more trouble, Ben, agreed?"

"Agreed," Ben said as they nodded to Mrs Davies and took their leave.

"Want to tell me what that was all about?" Abbey asked as she pulled away, noticing the curtain twitching on departure as it did on arrival.

"What what was about?" Ethan replied, perplexed.

"Okay, let's play it like that then shall we," Abbey said,

exasperated. "I'll ask you three questions, no more, no less. And you have to answer honestly."

"I'm hurt you think I'd do anything less," Ethan said, looking out of the window, away from Abbey's accusatory glare.

"Why did we go out of our way to tell a mother her son would face no charges, when we'd given her no former impression that he would?"

"Did it not feel good doing just that?" Ethan asked. "How often do you get to make others, and by consequence yourself feel better?"

"Hmm. How did Mrs Davies's partner hurt his finger while he was making tea?" Abbey said mockingly.

"Accident prone, caught it on the kettle as it was boiling," Ethan offered bluntly.

"That's two," Ethan continued, filling the silence, and prompting the third question.

"Well do I dare ask. What was the text message you got?" Abbey concluded.

"It was from Johnson. I asked him to look into a couple of bits for me. He was confirming that Mr Lindon was on shift at the time of each of the copycats. With the exception of the first non-murder if you will."

"And?" Abbey probed.

"And, he was part of the team that resuscitated Harry on both occasions."

CHAPTER FORTY

"Mike, come in, Mike," the radio crackled on the dashboard, "we've got an urgent call-in for Tom."

"I'm a little busy back here at the moment," Tom shouted through the open hatch from the back of the ambulance, holding his wide stance for balance as he tried to secure the IV, all the while dealing with the motion of Mike weaving his way through the parting traffic.

Mike picked up the radio as the crawl continued.

"On our way back anyway, Janet Any message I can give him?"

"Just more questions from the police for him. I'm guessing to do with the girl you brought in previously. She's not good," came the reply through the static.

Tom lifted his head in the back, knowing full well there could be no further questioning on a girl that hadn't moved a muscle since they last met outside of her room.

"Tell them that's a real good use of my time," Tom suggested.

"Hey, Janet, he'll be there. Do me a favour and make sure my subbie is good to go after my break."

Tom dropped the gurney from the ambulance and motioned that Mike move and allow him to deliver their latest casualty in what had already proven to be a very busy day.

"Not this time, Tom," Mike declared, "you know they're waiting for you inside. I'll drop her off. She'll be fine."

"Whatever," Tom said despondently, watching Mike check the sides were secured and head off to the building's entrance.

"You'll be back with me before you know it. Then you'll be wishing they'd needed you longer," Mike called over to his partner as he walked away.

Tom watched his partner disappear into the heart of the building, knowing full well that the casualty in front would be fine, needing nothing more than bedrest and at worst a couple of days' monitoring. He also knew Mike would be taking his break after delivering his patient just as he had confirmed. With the rest of the ambulance drop area quiet, Tom collected his personal belongings from the back of the bus, closed the doors and sidled around to the passenger side door. As expected upon opening the door he saw Mike's phone, wallet, ID and cigarettes riding shotgun.

"Fuck it," he said, drawing a cigarette from the packet and lighting it using the lighter always left in with the sticks. He'd always found it funny that the first thing Mike would do with a new pack would be to take out three or four and make room for his lighter.

Tom pocketed the cigarettes, closed the door and leant back on the side of the ambulance, blowing smoke in the air.

"You're lucky I'm so honest, partner," he said, pushing himself off the vehicle and making his way round to the main reception. "See you sometime."

CHAPTER FORTY-ONE

"Hospital just rang through. Mr Lindon will be making himself available to us this afternoon. He just got in from a call-out and needs to clean up first," Meadows informed his twosome currently kicking their heels in the incident room.

"On his own, or will we be speaking through legal counsel," Ethan asked.

"Hey, I'm just your PA, Mr Marshall. I shall be as surprised as you are when he walks through the door."

"No fuss about coming in though?" Abbey asked.

"It would appear not. But I'll repeat, you now know everything I do. The moment he walks through our doors, we shall all know more."

Reed moved around the apartment taking in the cleanliness, opening drawers and touching the gadgets within the kitchen, causing Tom to cringe with every tacky fingerprint left behind. Now wasn't the time to berate though, or for that matter show any sign of fallibility.

"Can we just do what we're here to do," Tom ventured.

"Nice place," Reed said, continuing his casual walk as if a prospective buyer.

"So what happened to remaining faceless?" Reed continued, coming back into view as he completed his rounds. "You not concerned I've seen your face?"

"Not even a little bit," Tom replied matter of factly. "Circumstance dictates everything. And maybe being so hands off previously has created this little predicament. We can save the light chit-chat for another time. We now know what each other looks like, it doesn't make me your BFF. How we progress is your call. For now, all you need to do is take the equipment in the study to this address," Tom finished, handing Reed a note and set of keys.

"Starting to sweat a little are ya," Reed teased.

Tom paused, weighing up the youth in front of him. He was without doubt that Reed would be a spiteful and vindictive individual given the slightest opportunity. However, as he was still of an age where bravado could mask fear, Tom hoped he really was as malicious as he appeared. Tom smiled, and stepped close to Reed, just inches separating them.

"To sweat would be to suggest emotion, and I've already told you I am devoid of that. If you are too, and you do show all the wonderful traits I admire in a person, then we can go on to do great things together. Great things," he whispered. "For a noose to tighten, they need a rope. All we're doing is making sure they don't find one to hand when they come looking. Come on," he said, stepping back and moving toward the study, "I've got somewhere I'm expected to be."

Reed sneered his approval and followed.

Tom made his way into the station having parked in one of the few visitors parking bays. A good sign, he reasoned. Taking in his surroundings and comparing the hurried activity of its incumbents to the hospital, he slalomed his way toward the front desk when he recognised the consultant from the previous hospital meeting waving and making his way through a crowd of his own to greet him.

"Mr Marshall," Tom stated, extending his hand, "what can I do for you?"

"Thanks for coming in, Mr Lindon," Ethan said, accepting the handshake.

"Not a problem, happy to help in any way I can. And please call me Tom."

"This way then, Tom," Ethan said, leading the way, "we're just down here. I hope it wasn't too much of an inconvenience for you. I understand we interrupted a shift."

"Nothing major. Day shift is always the quieter rota. Unless you catch a road traffic collision of course."

"Getting to see people on their worst day must be hard to take," Ethan said, blowing out his cheeks. "Here we are," Ethan continued, turning the handle of the interview room.

Abbey was already stood, leaning against the back wall as Ethan and Tom entered.

"Ms Swift," Tom commented, his face remaining expressionless.

"Detective Swift," she said with a smile.

"Please, take a seat," Ethan offered, gesturing to the single seat, ensuring Tom had no opportunity to try and fill one of the two on the opposite side. The room was set up in the same conditions as it would be for any other interrogation, with the exception of a tray sitting atop of the table bestowing a jug of iced water along with three tumbler glasses for its occupants.

"Do help yourself," he continued, taking his own seat.

"DI Swift," Ethan stated, looking at Abbey and gesturing to the chair next to him.

"I'm fine standing, thank you."

"Sit down, detective," Ethan instructed.

Ethan had been away from his previous consulting role for a little while, but not long enough to have forgotten how detectives used the interrogation rooms to their benefit. There was certainly an advantage to be gained, aiding on the pressuring of a suspect into confessing or providing information. And one of the easiest ways to exert pressure was to have the natural ability to appear bigger and loom large over an individual by standing tall or pacing the room as they forcibly sat on a chair, purposely sat low to the ground. This was not one of those occasions. This was going to be a case of seeing whether the man opposite them wanted to tell them anything. If they tried to be aggressive, Ethan knew that would be met with nothing but simple and stubborn resolve. It was about creating an opportunity, not catechising.

"Mr Lindon," Abbey managed as she took her seat, trying to hide her annoyance.

"Detective," Tom retorted with a wry grin.

"So what can I do for you?" Tom asked, taking control of the situation. "As I understand it, the girl has shown little sign of any improvement. Still struggling to find the guy?"

"It's more about looking back over the night it happened. If that's okay with you?" Ethan requested.

"Sure. Though over and above what I told you already, I'm not sure what I can offer."

"You said a guy," Abbey chipped in. "The girl had two flatmates, why'd you say guy?"

"Don't be so flippant," Tom snapped. "If it was one of the flatmates you'd have them in custody already... and I wouldn't be here trying to help you along, would I? I may not have witnessed as many scenes as yourself, Detective, but I know that the majority of crimes of that physical nature are perpetrated by men."

"Very true," Abbey confirmed, nodding her head, letting silence fill the room.

"We also understand that you got there only a short time after the attack itself took place. In fact, it's because of your swift response that the girl even stands a fighting chance," Ethan said, bringing the conversation back on topic.

"Not soon enough," Tom replied resignedly.

"Time will tell," Ethan concluded.

"Getting back to that night. You said when we spoke previously that the weather was horrendous, no reason for anyone to be out, if I recall correctly," Abbey stated.

"Sounds right," Tom confirmed.

"Right. And with the weather being as it was, anyone outside would've stood out, correct?"

"Correct," Tom agreed, wondering where this was going.

"And you also said that you didn't remember seeing a face, or a body for that matter standing out to you either on your way to the call, or when you got there."

"Not that I can recall," Tom stated, rubbing his thumb and forefinger across his eyes and bridge of his nose.

"Right, and that is understandable," Ethan ventured, leaning forward in his chair and joining in the conversation, "you'd have had a lot going on, and more important things to concentrate on."

"Exactly. Like I said, I'm not sure what more I can do to assist you."

"But," Abbey began, "then the doc here and I got talking, and often it's not until a memory is invoked somehow, that it can be correctly recollected. Way above my head, but all very interesting, wouldn't you say?" Abbey proposed.

"Very," Tom said with a heavy sigh.

"This," Abbey started, reaching into her jacket and pulling out three photographs. Abbey gave a quick glance to each of the pictures before placing two face down on the table next to her, and one in front of Tom, her finger tapping the image of the young man before them.

"This is Danny Jemson. Now... without putting words in your mouth, this is who we believe committed the assault on the night of your call-out. Does that bring back anything? Anything at all?"

Tom sat bored, rubbing a hand across the short stubble on his face.

"Nothing, no."

"Worth a shot," Ethan interjected. "A shame as we also think he may be responsible for a far more serious crime too."

"Same type of MO, mind," Abbey threw out. "Brutal and disorderly."

"Disorderly?" Tom asked, looking at the face-down photographs still to be revealed.

"Often happens when the accused is of lower intelligence," Ethan surmised.

"They get caught up in the moment you see," Abbey added, "I'm sure you must have seen it at some point, being what you are," she offered.

"What I am?"

"Sure, you must get call-outs even worse than the attack on the girl. A first responder, paramedic," Abbey concluded.

"I'm sure this all feels a little off-piste, Mr Lindon, but we feel there may be a common link between the crimes," Ethan continued, reaching over to the as yet unrevealed photographs, flipping them both over, creating a two-tier pyramid with Danny at the top. "If you can offer anything. Well, I'm sure you can understand that we'd all love to see some swift justice on this one."

Tom leaned forward to look at the two photographs, a glint of recognition that didn't go unnoticed by Ethan.

"And these are linked to another case you say?" Tom asked, again showing signs of tedium.

"There is that possibility, although we'll be just as happy to confirm that that isn't the case," Ethan confirmed.

"Do you recognise either?" Abbey asked.

"Should I? An old man, and a young boy. Would I have any reason to know either?"

"Not necessarily," Ethan offered apologetically. "I appreciate we've pulled you off shift for this. The boy's name is Benjamin. The man is Harry Murphy."

"I see a lot of old men, Mr Marshall, we may have crossed paths at some point, but it certainly raises no alarms. And the boy I've never met. I'm sorry. Are we done?"

"We are," Ethan said quickly as Abbey was about to speak, "thank you for your time, let me see you out."

"No need," Tom said sharply. "Thank you," he corrected softly, standing, nodding to Abbey who returned the gesture as he made his way out of the room.

Abbey waited for the door to click shut and a few seconds to pass for her own piece of mind before addressing Ethan.

"Why not push him on the description of the last attack?"

"Because it was better to let him leave thinking he hadn't given as much away as he had. Or reveal that we know more than we had indicated."

"So did he give you enough?" Abbey asked.

"More than. Why didn't he ask whether we'd caught Danny Jemson? Or at least had some line of progress."

"Because he doesn't care," Abbey offered.

"Because he knows full well where Mr Jemson is. He also couldn't hide the flash in his eyes when he had three recognisable individuals placed in front of him in one go. So he tried to stick to half-truths. He passed Harry off as a possibility as he knows we could check the records, and over a period of time link the two. He says he never met Ben, no doubt true also."

"And what was with all the arriving swiftly, and swift justice?" Abbey asked.

"Just to try and get a reaction. By association the word will trigger emotion, in the simple way he doesn't like you, he won't like the word being used in repetition."

"Glad to know I have a use!" Abbey said, grinning.

"Like it or not, he is an intelligent man. He won't like having any of his work questioned as we did with his first copy. If he has an endgame, we just sped it up."

"So now we have to wait for his next move... again?" she asked.

"Wait on that, and continue to try and find our greasy-haired mystery man."

CHAPTER FORTY-TWO

"Got a rope did they?" Reed sniggered.

"They've got nothing. But he knows. Which puts us in an interesting position," Tom replied.

"Us? Seems to me you're the one in an interesting position. They don't even know who I am."

"Yet. And you seem to be forgetting that I do. In fact, I know a whole lot more than you may realise, Reed Morgan. Born to a single mother, with a habit for the powder and the pound. Early years were a mix of visits to the hospital, no doubt from your whore mother's various men, and then more of the same after you were moved into foster care. Earning a reputation for being difficult you went from family to family, with yet more hospital visits thrown in. At eighteen, and legally an adult, you took it upon yourself to move back in at home. Since which time the only visits to the hospital have been for your mother. Doesn't seem like she would be having many male suitors around these days though, Reed. So who is it causing her harm I wonder? You think I wouldn't do my research? Surely I never gave you that impression. Like I said, this doesn't make us friends, but I can assure you, you don't want me as an enemy."

Reed grunted and turned his attention to their surroundings.

"Whatever, man. So what is this place?"

The building in front of them was as close to derelict as a property still in use could be. They'd parked the car on the sparse gravel out front, having travelled up a well-worn tree-lined driveway to get there. Acres of land ran off in every direction and the nearest neighbouring property could only be seen at some point on the horizon. The sun was already starting to set and for the first time Reed had found himself putting his guard up, being alone in such a remote location.

"Home, Mr Morgan. This is where I grew up. And it's also where I'm going to see out my days."

"Sounds like you're getting ready to give up, to me. I thought you said they had nothing," Reed stated.

Tom stared hard at Reed and moved so they were face to face with only inches between them, a mix of a boxers' weigh-in establishing dominance and a father passing on a secret to his favoured son.

"You still don't get it, do you?" Tom whispered. "It's not about me. It's about the work. The work must continue. And if I am to be caught, be it today, tomorrow, or even years from now, it was always going to be on my terms. And my terms will dictate both when and how."

Tom backed away and started towards the property.

"Come on," he called, "there's preparation to be done."

CHAPTER FORTY-THREE

Jameson was already in the incident room with Superintendent Meadows when Abbey and Ethan walked in.

"Sir, Irish," Abbey said with a grin.

"Hey, Tony, something happened?" Ethan asked.

The room felt different with just the four of them filling the space. With the lack of the usual commotion, all attention seemed to converge on the whiteboard at the front of the room and created a more morose atmosphere, highlighting the full extent of the grave situation they were a part of. On the left-hand side of the board, four lifeless faces looked back at them offering little assistance, but seemingly asking for answers of their own. On the right-hand side, two more pictures were pinned, although they were at least live-action pictures. In the middle a stock photo from Tom Lindon's personnel file sat above a sketch artist's impression of his unknown partner.

Jameson moved forward and tapped the picture on the right of a young woman smiling fondly for the camera in the summer sun.

"Another you'll need to move over, I'm afraid. Found out last night that she didn't make it."

Silence filled the air again as Ethan and Abbey took in the news.

"At least she gets the nice pic on the board, eh?" Abbey said.

"She's not one of our victims. Not really," Ethan offered. "Mr Jemson may be her killer, but this was his murder. He got a taste for it and went rogue. And paid the price for doing so."

"I don't think there was ever an intent to include the girl," Jameson said.

"Yet here she is though," Abbey replied.

"Most bizarre board I've seen in a while. It's all so contradictory," Meadows added.

"It's not bizarre, it's fucked up," Abbey argued, walking over to address the board and her small audience. She worked her way down the left-hand side, pointing at each picture in turn.

"This guy, Mr Arthur Green, already dead. But still a victim. Nobody deserves that. We know Danny Jemson killed Lisa Cole, and we're happy to call him a victim too."

"Not happy to," Ethan countered.

"Looks that way to me," Abbey said, "yet we have a young girl, Susan Fisher, killed before she even had a chance to live her life, who we say isn't a victim."

Abbey turned her attention to the two pictures in the middle.

"We're as sure as can be that this grease monkey is responsible for killing our homeless victim, Stewart. And yet we still have no idea who he is. And then, even better, we believe this degenerate is responsible for the whole thing and can't really be sure that he has killed anyone. That a decent enough summary of where we are?" Abbey vented.

The three men before her all looked to the floor, unable to meet Abbey's plea for answers.

"In a nutshell," Ethan managed.

"Not entirely," Meadows muttered. "That print on the eggshell came back as a dead end too. Nothing in the system."

"So, fucking with us then," Abbey stated.

"We watching him at least?" Ethan asked the superintendent.

"Got uniforms watching his apartment, but he's not been back it would appear, since he left here. And taken holiday due from work too. So at the moment..."

"Not so much," Ethan concluded.

"Not so much," Meadows agreed.

A double knock on the incident-room door prevented the return of the uncomfortable silence of no one having the answers they all sought.

"Sorry to intrude," Adam offered as he pushed the door open, "we've got some activity I think you're going to want to see."

Ethan, Abbey and Meadows arrived back into an empty IT centre with Adam.

"Where is everyone?" Abbey asked.

"Didn't think it was appropriate," Adam replied. "The information is twofold, and the five D's only know half of it."

"Come on then, Adam, let us have it," Meadows said.

"Okay. Well, first off, I don't know how he's escalated from the website contacts to personal email, and I probably never will, but we identified a file as potential junk that was intended for Superintendent Meadows' account."

"From?" Meadows demanded.

"Better that I show you," Adam replied, moving over to the central console.

The three of them huddled in behind Adam as his fingers flew around the keyboard with ease and at lightning speed, sending instructions and getting instant responses as numerous pages opened before them.

"Right then. Like I said, this came into the superintendent, and has a zip file attached. That then went through all our security checks to verify it was virus free. Once that was done, as it came from an unrecognised account it was flagged by *Beth* for further investigation, and when we open it... You get this..." Adam explained, double-clicking the file as he turned to gauge his guests' reactions.

All three had a look of surprise and curiosity as hundreds of documents opened up as if flying from within the screen to the front, shortly overlapped by the next mix of newspaper and internet headlines, webpage stories and hand-typed messages.

"What the fu...?" Abbey started.

"It's all about me?" Ethan affirmed.

"Rate yourself, Doc," Abbey teased.

Ethan smiled, but remained concentrated on the screen before them.

"No, it is literally all about me," he repeated. "These are all stories and headlines from cases I've previously been involved in, or about killers I would've studied and lectured on. No doubt they are in for filler, and to help create the full effect which can only be done by having so many documents."

"Agreed," Adam said. "That wouldn't be nearly as impressive aesthetically with a dozen sheets to sift through."

"And are we sifting through it?" Meadows asked.

"Done and done," Adam confirmed, tapping away once more on the keyboard.

As he did so, the papers appeared to sort themselves into separate piles on the screen as they continued to watch.

"Pile one," Adam began, "is any story that makes reference to the good doctor. Pile two is anything that appears as a hand-typed document or email, and pile three is a collection of all and sundry that relates to other crimes and serial killers. Which, confirming your filler theory, is by far and away the biggest contributor to the overall zip file."

"Which we can therefore disregard," Ethan said.

"What's in pile one then?" Abbey asked.

"Exactly as I said, any newspaper or website that ever filed a report with a mention of Dr Ethan Marshall. All unedited, bar one."

Adam again took control of the screen, swiping documents away with the mouse until he found the article headline he was looking for.

ALWAYS SOMEONE CLOSE WHO PAYS THE PRICE

"This one was..." Adam offered.

"An article in the *Telegraph*," Ethan interrupted. "It was after the Railway Killer trial. This was a follow-up piece after Emily..."

"We don't need to go into detail," Meadows interjected.

"It was in red," Ethan said.

"What was?" Abbey asked.

"The headline," he replied.

"Correct," Adam said. "That's all we found though, everything else is as it was printed, so I don't know if this was a formatting error or..."

"It's not an error," Ethan said, "it's a warning. Tony, I think we need to talk."

"I need to show you this first then," Adam insisted. "That was the only change in that one, and pile two was only two documents. The first is just a copy of his original contact and taunt. And the second is the confession of the woman, written before she shot Mrs Marshall."

"So?" Abbey asked on everyone's behalf.

"I need to show you what came up from the forum fishing expedition."

Adam worked his magic on the workstation once more, shutting down the information already covered and opening up several screen grabs from the forum they had all come to recognise.

"Take a look at the third screenshot," Adam instructed.

Sudo:So still no Clown?

Jags:Guess we're not worthy of him anymore. His hero hasn't been around much.

Tutor:I'm still here.

Slash:Oh, look who's back. Found some more bullshit to peddle?

"This was just yesterday," Adam explained, becoming the centre of attention again. "He hasn't been on since your homeless victim was discovered. Not even in the background. Then we have a bit more trash talk with him silent, but take a look at the fifth screenshot when he comes back into the conversation."

Tutor:You're not a believer, Slash. I can respect that. And why should you be without proof?

Slash:Exactly. Finally we can agree on something.

Sudo:So make him believe, Tutor.

Jags:Yeah, make him bleed! LOL.

Tutor:No need for that, Jags. I bear no ill will to my contemporaries. However, I will include you, and ask you to look out for an event in the evening two days from now 51.4912, 0.2237. Think Jack the Stripper.

Slash:Ha! Can't even get that right. You, sir, are no better than Clown, and a waste of our time.

"The abuse and backlash then carries on for a bit, but he logged off, presumably disinterested," Adam concluded.

"So what are the numbers?" Abbey asked, "and why would he get the moniker wrong?"

"He didn't," Ethan said. "Jack the Stripper was a killer from the sixties. He was known to take prostitutes, strip them naked having strangled or drowned them and dump their bodies in the Hammersmith area by the river."

"And those numbers look like co-ordinates," Meadows suggested.

"This isn't right, Tony. This is for us, not for them. A single location, on a specific date."

"You know we can't ignore this, Ethan."

"It's an open invitation. God knows what will actually happen. But it won't be the conclusion. This doesn't end this way," Ethan stated.

"Gift horse, Ethan. And we're gonna have to follow it. This is from yesterday. That gives us plenty of time to review the location, and then be there ready on the night. No surprises."

Ethan shook his head and sighed heavily.

"You know that's not gonna be the case."

"Come on, Doc," Abbey enthused, "let's finish this."

"I need to talk to you now," Ethan said to Meadows, ignoring Abbey.

Abbey closed the door and took a seat beside Ethan with a face like thunder, crossing her arms ostentatiously and facing Superintendent Meadows who was sat opposite with both arms behind his head, pondering as he chewed the inside of his lip.

"This is bollocks," Abbey fumed.

"I just think it makes sense to take every precaution. If he thinks that the best way of coming after me is through another, then we have to reduce that pool," Ethan explained.

"And why wouldn't that be your family?" Abbey continued.

Meadows shot a look at Abbey that stopped any further comments following in the immediate future.

"I'm sorry," Abbey offered, "I didn't mean..."

"It's fine. They would be the immediate concern and that was my first thought. But Tony's taking care of that. And I can't see how he'd get the information to put them in danger. This is reactionary, not planned. It'll be a direct relationship," Ethan said, "and he only knows of one."

"Well, he can fuck off if he thinks he's getting me removed from this case."

"He's not removing you... I am," Meadows ordered, "and it's not a discussion."

"What?"

"It's the right thing to do, Abbey," Ethan said.

"So the doc's gonna fly solo is he?"

"Jameson can partner up while this gets sorted," Meadows instructed.

Abbey looked from Meadows to Ethan, unable to put her anger into words or knowing who to take her frustrations out on. With nothing coming back other than a look from her superintendent daring her to question his decision, Abbey took her leave from the room ensuring she slammed the door on her way out.

CHAPTER FORTY-FOUR

Abbey sat on her sofa clutching a cushion tightly as far away as possible from Ethan as he made his way through an evening meal of beans on toast, eating from a lap tray while watching the latest evening quiz show.

"Full pay and you get to be at home. People would kill for less," Ethan said.

"Do I look like a bloody gardener to you?" Abbey replied, grabbing the TV remote and turning the volume up.

"Which South African golfer won the Masters in 2011?"

"Ernie Els," Abbey offered quickly.

"Schwartzel," Ethan corrected, with a shake of the head through a mouthful of beans.

"Charl Schwartzel was who we were looking for."

Ethan smiled to himself while Abbey stared over and shook her head.

"So having a gambling habit helps."

"If you say so."

"What is the world's largest landlocked country?"

"Kazakhstan," Ethan answered instantly.

Abbey looked over as the television confirmed his answer.

"It wasn't done out of spite, Abbey."

"I'm a big girl, Ethan. I can look after myself."

"You need to know when to let people help you, Abbey. You're not as tough as you think you are."

"Don't try and doc me, Doc."

"Why would I? You don't need any help, right?"

CHAPTER FORTY-FIVE

Ethan and Jameson stood in the middle of what was once an industrial warehousing hub, silently taking in the current activity, while three plain-clothes officers walked the perimeter looking in through the windows as best they could. With the amount of graffiti and boarding up against the buildings this was no easy task. A group of young adolescents were at the far end of the now redundant parking lots, killing time with their skateboards, and who knows what else. They had become instantly suspicious of the bodies invading their space and all the boastful shouts that had been heard as they entered the estate had long disappeared. Ethan watched as they kept looking over to an older, no doubt ringleader, sat on his own staring directly at Ethan with a knowing smirk, adjusting his cap and throwing shade over his face.

"You see this fitting?" Ethan asked.

"Don't look at me. I'm just along for the ride," Jameson replied.

"Don't remind me."

"Still pissed then?"

"What do you think?"

Jameson went to speak but Ethan held up a hand and shook his head as one of the officers broke away from the building's edge to join them, making sure not to turn his back fully on the group at the far end.

"He seems to have taken a liking to you," the officer offered as the ringleader's grin grew, throwing a nod of acknowledgement of the two-way appraisal that was taking place between him and Ethan.

"Better than him urinating around his group and the estate I guess," Ethan replied. "What do you think?" he asked, glancing over at the two other officers still doing the rounds.

"Nothing untoward. No obvious break-ins. This place is as it has been since the last business upped sticks as far as we can tell."

"Which unfortunately would make it fit for purpose," Ethan surmised, taking another look around at his derelict surroundings. "I just don't see it though."

Jameson tapped Ethan on the arm as the group of youths had now come to a complete stop, weighing up the adult invasion of their space, still every so often glancing over to side with their loner accomplice.

"Think they could've seen anything?" Jameson asked.

"Can't hurt to ask, eh?" the officer said, and sighed, signalling for his two colleagues to join him as they approached the group with caution.

Ethan's concentration fixed on the older member of the group who had started nervously flicking his own attention from the approaching threesome back to Ethan and Jameson who remained where they stood.

"What's got to him do you think?"

"Looks like we may be about to find out," Jameson replied.

The older member stood up, instantly gaining the attention of everyone.

He now looked far older than the teenage skateboarders who were all waiting to see what was going to happen as much as the officers in attendance.

Enjoying the attention, the man made a show of taking off his cap and letting his long matted black hair fall down as he locked eyes once again with Ethan, raised his eyebrows, and silently mouthed, "Fucking pigs." With that he turned and took off down a side alley at pace, leaving the officers wondering what to do and who to turn their attention to.

Time seemed to slow as Ethan and Jameson watched the scene before them play out, before Ethan suddenly sprung into a sprint, chasing in the direction of their escapee, calling back behind him as he went. "Stay here and find out who he is and how those kids know him."

Ethan knew that the man only had a few seconds' head start in reality but if he had taken a number of turns before he reached the alleyway then the chase would be in vain before it had even begun. As he reached the turning, however, he saw a body dart left less than fifty yards ahead of him. Reed looked back over his shoulder as he turned, that same grin on his face, eyes flashing with excitement as the adrenaline pushed him on. Ethan knew from the earlier description who he was in pursuit of. He also knew he had well over ten years on him and in a foot race that was never a benefit. Experience counted for little in a sprint. He was in good physical shape though and felt that he was closing in as he took the same left turn and saw the man pushing bins to the floor as he passed them to both hinder Ethan and aid his escape. Ethan pushed himself harder, avoiding the minor debris that had been left in his way and continued to close the gap as Reed took two quick turns between buildings.

Well, he certainly knows the area, Ethan thought to himself as he raced on, feeling more and more like he was being led around a labyrinth that only one of them had previously had a chance to map out.

Ethan got the impression that Reed seemed to be ensuring that he was kept at a safe distance, yet just far enough to keep him interested. Reed glanced back at him and visibly slowed down, seemingly considering the next move of his getaway. Ethan saw him make yet another turn but with the added incentive that he seemed to be slowing further and feeling the pressure of the chase as there was now very little gap between them. Taking the turn, Ethan instinctively stopped in his tracks as Tom's collaborator stood sneering before him in the middle of a walled enclosure.

"Not bad for an old boy," Reed offered.

"Your approval means everything to me too, as I'm sure you can imagine," Ethan replied, breathing heavily.

Reed tutted and spat to the side as he filled his lungs with deep breaths of his own.

"I'll see you soon then," Reed said, as he turned and sprinted towards the wall at the end of the alleyway.

Ethan had already anticipated that there was only one way this could play out if the young man expected to be leaving of his own accord, having intentionally boxed himself in as he had. Without the need to turn, Ethan had shocked Reed with his speed from a standing start and was almost on top of him as he sprung off his right leg and started to scramble up and over the wall. Reed had got both arms on top and was in the process of dragging himself over when he felt an opposite force tug sharply on the cuff of his left leg trying to pull him back down as Ethan scrambled to get a grip on him. Pain shot through Reed's jaw as the reverse motion meant that his chin crashed into the brickwork he was fighting to overcome. As rage took over, Reed kicked his legs violently, trying to free himself. With the extra convulsions Ethan was unable to get a hold of the second leg and could only look up as Reed lifted his right foot and drove it directly into Ethan's face, sending him crashing to the ground as Reed made his final pull over the wall, offering a miniature salute to Ethan's prone body below him.

CHAPTER FORTY-SIX

Ethan sat opposite Meadows, an ice pack held across the right side of his face hiding the majority of the bruising and swelling that had come up at some point between Reed taking his final cocky leave over the wall and the rest of the team finding him in a semi-conscious state.

"You get a face like that, you should at least be paid well to do so," Meadows commented, gesturing at his picture of Mike Tyson mid-swing over a bandy-legged Trevor Berbick.

"Please don't give him that kind of credit," Ethan groaned. "I should never have stopped. I should have carried on running round that corner and we'd be having a very different conversation."

"Or you wouldn't be here to have a conversation at all. Believe it or not, Ethan, this isn't the worst outcome you could have faced!" Meadows snapped. "You're not here to be literally chasing down the bad guys."

"Noted," Ethan said, removing the ice pack and stretching his jaw, before wincing as he gingerly replaced the pack over the damage.

"The kids didn't even know him," Ethan continued. "They were just as suspicious of him as they were of us."

"So will anything happen now?" Meadows asked.

"I doubt it was ever going to. They were seeing if we bit."

"Which we did. And now we have no choice but to follow through. I don't like this, Ethan."

"It's no more than bravado. Letting us know that we're still on his timetable."

"His or theirs?"

"His. There may be more than one involved, but there is only one in charge," Ethan confirmed.

"So in the meantime?"

"In the meantime we spin our wheels and wait for tomorrow night."

Reed walked around what at some stage was the living room of an impressive property, picking up the random items layered in dust still adorning the shelves along two of the four walls.

"Decided against redecorating then did you?" Reed taunted.

"I'm not here to turn a profit, Reed," Tom replied as he worked in the corner of the room, filling wooden crates with various tools and rope. "This isn't a doer-upper. And I'm not asking you to stay here. So why don't you just tell me what I need to know?"

"Easy, man. I'm just playing. Don't you know you're supposed to try and enjoy your work? You're there more than anywhere else. Did you know that? Messed up, right?"

"Not to be discourteous, or judgemental, but when was the last time you fucking worked, Reed? I mean, really grafted?"

"How about yesterday. Doing your fucking donkey work. How about you try and do this without me, you ungrateful..." Reed stated defensively.

"Okay, okay," Tom interrupted, chuckling, "no need to get all het up. And it's not donkey work. You're far more important than that."

Tom got to his feet and walked over to address his partner, tapping his cheek as he did so.

Reed cooled his temper instantly, his body lifting with pride at the scrap of praise offered.

"You're the heir apparent, Reed. And your day is coming soon. Now tell me, how'd we get on?"

"As you said. They did the rounds. Looked the site over."

"And Mr Marshall?" Tom asked.

"He'll have a sore face this morning, but he'll live."

"On his own?"

"There were three pigs checking everything. Him and a bigger guy just stood in the middle, trying to look like they owned the place. Had me down as running with a bunch of kids. Maybe he's not all that after all?"

"I wouldn't underestimate him if I were you. But he's not the only one who can read people. He may see himself as noble, but I'd call it nothing more than predictable."

Tom turned back to the boxes in the corner, stacking them into pairs.

"Come on, Mr Morgan. Grab those and bring them out to the barn. Things are about to get interesting."

CHAPTER FORTY-SEVEN

"I've never been good at these," Jameson offered, breaking the silence.

Ethan looked out over the same forecourt they had been at just the day before, only this time the atmosphere had changed due to the effect of the night setting and its natural mood lighting along with the raised stakes and feeling of anticipation. They had breached the protective boardings and taken residence in one of the defunct buildings earlier in the day, confident that, at that point at least, they were alone. To his right, stood at the next window, the tactical leader of Operation Nightfall remained motionless, sighing at Jameson's input. Frank Emmerson had overseen countless strategic manoeuvres in his time with both the armed forces and then the police during his thirty years of service and the one thing he always knew to be true was it was a specific skill set. The second thing he believed from experience was those without that skill, either naturally or taught, were a hindrance and put him and his team in danger. Detectives were at the top of his list of those hindrances. They had their own specific talents, and certainly wouldn't want him putting himself into one of their investigations. But here he was, stuck in a room with a fidgety case substitute, and a doctor. You couldn't make it up!

"It's the waiting. It's just not me. I need to be doing something," Jameson continued nervously.

Their room for the evening was layered with dust across the worn carpet tiles and remains of office furniture not wanted by those either vacating for pastures new or failing to the pressures of the economy. The three bodies lying prone on the surrounding rooftops could barely be picked out by those who knew where to look, and even then, there was no way to identify that they were armed and taking dead aim at the centre point before them.

"No visible movement. Red?" Frank checked in over his radio.

"No visible movement," came the reply.

"Green... Blue?"

"No visible movement."

"All quiet."

"We expecting anything?" Frank asked, turning to Ethan and Jameson.

"I thought we might see some unsuspecting hangers on. But maybe even they had better things to do with their time tonight," Ethan concluded.

"You got a time limit on this?" Frank asked.

"No."

"Then we wait."

Silence filled the room once more as Frank turned his attention back to the scene before him, waiting for it to play out.

"It's bullshit is what it is," Abbey huffed, continuing her tirade against Ethan, her current position and the senior brass that enforced her self-containment and boredom.

Abbey sat huddled at one end of her sofa, phone in one hand, a glass of wine in the other as she watched the muted TV screen play out silent music videos from individuals and bands she'd never heard of, wondering when she'd aged so suddenly.

"Is it?" Lucy chimed in on cue.

She had let Abbey put the world to rights for over twenty minutes and was starting to bore of acting the dutiful friend, agreeing with all and sundry as Abbey vented.

"Or..." she offered.

"Or nothing. Don't you dare 'or' me, Luce," Abbey interrupted, raising her voice.

"No you're right, Abs. None of this has been done with your best interests at the forefront of Ethan and the superintendent's thinking. In fact, they probably think you're such a liability that you'll never get another case again. Bleeding hearts of the world unite, Abbey Swift is having a bad day."

Abbey snorted, coughing wine back into her glass as she did so.

"Fuck's sake, Luce, you nearly made me spill my wine! I am allowed a little rant aren't I? If I can't feel sorry for myself with you, what's the point in a best friend?" Abbey laughed down the phone.

"Oh, I don't know. Maybe so they can tell you when you're becoming a pain in the arse and acting just a little too precious?" Lucy countered.

"You are brutal, you know that," Abbey replied.

"It's why you love me, no?"

Before Abbey could reply, their conversation was interrupted by a ring of the front doorbell. Abbey placed her wine on the table and made her way into the hallway, talking to Lucy as she went.

"One minute, hun, I've got guests."

"A party with no invite, I'm hurt."

"Not invited guests, doughnut. Give me two minutes," Abbey said, placing the phone down on the shoe rack as she opened the door to her visitor.

Abbey opened the door only to be surprised by the pizza delivery man stood before her looking around the neighbourhood in a carefree fashion.

"As much as I'd love to tell you different, I think you've got the wrong house," she said to the man.

"Swift," he responded, checking a ticket attached to the box, all the while chewing on his gum. "Large Hawaiian, extra mushrooms?"

Abbey looked slightly confused, thrown by the man addressing her by name.

"That's me," she replied, "but I didn't..."

With a quick look over his shoulder to reassure himself that the street remained quiet, Reed rushed forward, thrusting the pizza box toward Abbey's abdomen. As Abbey instinctively grabbed for the box, Reed threw a fierce overhand right, hitting hard downward into Abbey's jaw, sending her sprawling back into the hallway. Reed walked through the front door, closing it behind him, calmly stalking his target as Abbey pushed herself backwards, scrambling for safety, unable to gain control of her legs.

Looking up as Reed stood high above her, now appearing far more imposing than he had done just a minute before, Abbey rolled onto all fours and started to crawl toward the kitchen, looking for anything within reach that she could use to defend herself. Reed's smirk grew as he slowly followed his prey, enjoying the moment.

"Here kitty, kitty, kitty," Reed goaded.

"Fuck you," Abbey managed as she could feel her scrambled brain slowly regaining control of her body.

"Oh honey, that's only gonna be part of the fun."

Abbey's crawl quickened as she managed to get herself back to her feet of sorts, now almost on fingers and toes, galloping towards the kitchen that could provide an arsenal of weaponry.

Reed dashed forward, jumping on his quarry and stopping her in her tracks as she floundered below him with all the energy she could muster.

With the weight of him upon her, Abbey realised that the anticipated safety of the kitchen might as well be miles away, rather than the few metres it truly was.

"I knew you'd like it rough. I bet you're a screamer," Reed whispered breathily, leaning in next to Abbey's ear.

"You've no idea," Abbey managed through gritted teeth as she threw her head back violently, crashing into her assailant's nose.

Reed screamed out in agony as he simultaneously felt the dampness on his face and the taste of copper down his throat.

"HELP ME!" Abbey screamed at the top of her lungs as she continued to buck wildly.

Reed instinctively clasped a hand around Abbey's mouth giving her the opportunity to sink her teeth deep into two of his fingers, drawing yet more blood as he scrambled for purchase to silence the noise.

"Bitch!" Reed wailed.

Reed snatched his hand back to relative safety, ignoring the bloody mess as he grabbed Abbey by the hair and drove her face first into the floor sending her body limp.

"I knew you'd be a game girl," Reed managed as his sweat-soaked body sagged, sitting astride his prize.

Frank stood unmoved at the window in a state of constant awareness. There wasn't a movement of vermin or a change in wind direction that went unnoticed. Every little modification could mean a recalculation of the plan and how this might play out should the need arise. Ethan and Jameson continued to look out from their own viewpoints also, but without the ability to hold a hypervigilant state, unable to hide the despondency in the evening's activities, or lack thereof.

"It's your show, Mr Marshall. You call it," Frank said without any hint of movement.

"Well, I'm calling it. There's nothing to be gained here."

"Can't argue with that," Jameson agreed, stretching out his back and legs as his phone started ringing.

"Red, Green, Blue. We're done here," Frank informed, getting back on his radio comms. "Alpha, time to go home."

Ethan watched as the three roof-mounted silhouettes raised themselves up, packing up their equipment under the light of the moon. While they made their descent, the previously unseen ten-strong tactical unit made their way out from behind the various hoardings in their pairs onto the silent concourse. The estate now as busy with life as it had been all evening.

"I'd better call Abbey, and let her know," Ethan said, taking his phone from his pocket and making his way into the darkness of the room.

"Hold on, Ethan," Jameson called. "We need to get back to the station. They've been in contact again."

"No answer anyway," Ethan offered, putting his mobile back into his pocket.

CHAPTER FORTY-EIGHT

Ethan and Jameson walked back into a hub of activity as they entered the incident room. Bodies were racing around the room and manning the phones, giving and taking instructions at pace.

"Must've had a better night than us," Jameson assumed, taking his leave, with Ethan seeking out a familiar face.

Meadows and Adam were hunched over the table by the original whiteboard which now had a secondary board set up next to it, deep in a conversation which stopped abruptly as the superintendent spotted Ethan making his way through the crowd.

"Well, this looks promising," Ethan said with a smile. "Do you know something I don't?"

"I think we need to head outside for a minute," Meadows replied, walking and taking a firm grip of Ethan's arm.

At that point, however, Ethan's entire body felt like stone, an unmovable object, as his stomach dropped, and he took in the information and full horror of what lay before him on the secondary incident board. A blown-up picture of a battered and bruised Abbey showed her suspended by her feet from a beam in what appeared to be an old barn. The photo had been deliberately dated by being printed off in sepia, matching a secondary picture that was pinned next to it of an old farmhouse. Abbey's clothes were torn in several places and blood trailed in a thin stream from her mouth back towards her left eye. Although beaten physically, her eyes still burned with defiance and stared directly into the lens, capturing her situation. Next to the photo was another printout of what seemed to be a letter or email. The other half of the board was a mess of notations made in various coloured marker pens. At this stage it appeared there were no wrong answers in unravelling what had become a puzzle of desperation, only that the right answer lay within what had been transcribed before them, somewhere.

"When did... How?" Ethan stumbled. "Tony, we need to do something!"

"I'm so sorry, Ethan," Meadows managed.

"When did this come in?" Ethan asked, freeing his arm and moving before the board to study it in more detail.

"While you were watching the site," Adam replied.

"Ethan, we've got bodies at Swift's place as we speak."

"A bit late for that don't you think!" Ethan snapped.

"There are signs of a struggle, but nothing to suggest anything more than that at this stage," Meadows concluded.

"There at least," Jameson said, joining them at the board.

Ethan shook his head, pointing at the picture of Abbey before them, fighting against the bile in his stomach trying to make its way upward.

"So we consider that is her having come to no harm do we?" Ethan said, rubbing a hand across his face and pinching the bridge of his nose.

"Lindon was on shift, Ethan," Meadows continued. "We've requested he come in again when he clocks out."

"He won't," Ethan said, moving forward to look at the picture of the property on the board. "Where did he grow up?"

"Lindon?" Meadows replied. "No idea. Is that relevant?"

"It's where he's going. And it's where Abbey will be."

"How do you know that, Ethan? He could've taken her anywhere," Jameson said.

"You see the house? That's Ed Gein's house. It's where he took his victims. He hung them upside down like a huntsman would... And then he skinned them."

"Shit!" Adam managed in a whisper.

"He will have grown up somewhere similar," Ethan concluded. "Isolated at least. We need his life on a page, Tony. And somebody should be trying to contact his parents."

"On it," Adam offered, grabbing his belongings from the table and finding a corner where he could open up his laptop and get to work.

"And what he can't get I should be able to get from hospital records," Jameson said.

"Do it now, Irish," Meadows ordered, "and if he's still on site, I want him detained immediately."

Jameson nodded and headed off.

"We'll get her back, Ethan."

"He won't do anything until we're there," Ethan replied. "This is how it ends."

CHAPTER FORTY-NINE

Reed sat on one of the overturned crates, a malicious grin filling his narrow features as he watched Abbey swing gently under her own weight. Tom, meanwhile, stood staring out between the slats of the outhouse back down the driveway of the property, an old hunting rifle resting on its butt by his side. A trail of red lights flickered brightly in the distance as traffic made its way along the passing and surrounding roads. Everyday people making their way home after their workdays had been completed, oblivious to the work undertaken by others outside of their own daily bubble. With her hands bound, Abbey managed to flick a middle finger with a sarcastic smile at Reed who made his way with a sneer over to the viewing point alongside Tom.

"So now we're inviting guests?" he asked.

"Feel free to leave if you don't have the stomach for it."

"I thought you said the best ones never get caught?"

"Everyone gets caught," Abbey managed with a laugh, "especially two dipshits like you. Thinking you're something special, or different to any of the countless other delusional twats that *hear the voices...* or have *work to complete*."

"The best ones are the ones people remember," Tom explained, concentrating on the world outside. "I'll be remembered."

Abbey lifted herself by her stomach, grabbing at her feet, her bound hands flailing at the rope securing her in place, gaining nothing but a large shard of wood from the beam as she crashed back down toward the floor, swinging uncontrollably and screaming out in pain as the snap of her weight extended all the muscles in her legs further than naturally possible.

"Bitch!" Reed shouted as his attention was drawn back to the swinging piñata.

Reed advanced menacingly on Abbey who managed to slide the shard into a trouser pocket as she put her arms up in defensive mode just in time before a wide arcing kick at her head came crashing into her forearms and sent her swinging violently from side to side. Reed looked down at Abbey with her guard up and drove a straight kick into her midsection, taking the air and fight out of her on impact. Reed wound up for a punch to the same area but his arm was grabbed forcibly by Tom, the shotgun in his other hand pointing at the floor.

"Not now."

"Then when?" Reed asked, shrugging away and spitting onto Abbey.

Tom ignored the question and moved back to his concealed viewpoint.

"And stay away from the window, they need to see her."

Ethan and Meadows stood silently at the base of the drive, looking up at the silhouette of the outhouse, light creeping out of the breaks in the side panelling and roof as the tactical team, almost invisible to the naked eye, advanced on the property.

"Irish confirmed it. He clocked in all right, but then

switched to an on-site shift, feeling unwell. Needless to say, no one has seen him since."

Ethan just nodded, looking from the centre of everyone's attention to the surrounding geography and how it could still influence their as yet undetermined future.

"He chose this place for a reason," Ethan said. "He may have accepted this as his final stand, but he'll still have given himself an out, an option or possibility at least."

"What option?" Meadows countered. "Even if he were to escape from here, the whole of the Met, hell, the whole of the country's police force will know who he is. There's no out, Ethan!"

"This isn't a wait it out situation, Tony. The longer we wait, the greater danger Abbey is in."

"And him," Meadows replied as his radio crackled into life.

"Eyes on. Swift is suspended but conscious. No sign of unfriendlies. Hold positions."

Meadows snatched up his radio. "I want thirty-second updates... And any changes immediately," he snapped.

"Understood."

"He's not stupid, Tony. But I can tell you this, he won't go quietly, and if he sees he's going at all, he won't be going alone. The minimum impression he will want to leave is the pain of others."

"Swift," Meadows interrupted.

"That's the physical opportunity he's created. But the emotional impact spreads far greater. That's what will really be driving him. He'll want the column inches, and nothing guarantees that more than a final stand with a cop or two falling in the line of duty."

Tom continued to look out from his position, watching the shadows slowly closing in. Knowing that the climax was now a foregone conclusion, he breathed steadily in and out, calming the rising adrenaline against nature's fight or flight reaction.

"They here then?" Reed asked, rising up from his seated position back on the crate, careful not to fill the eyeline on Abbey supplied by the window.

"They are."

"So now what? We gonna kill her? Or you planning on taking them all on with a shotgun?"

Tom turned and stared derisively at Reed, shaking his head before turning his attention back to the building tension out front.

"You know your problem, Reed? You don't look at the big picture. The long game. You're all about the moment."

"Fuck you. You're the one who's backed us into shit creek alley. Where the fuck do we go from here? Why am I even here?"

"Time," Tom replied calmly. "You are here for time."

Tom turned away from the wall, swinging the shotgun up sharply as he did so, striding directly across to the windowpane and firing the gun from hip height, sending two shots straight into the central mass offered by Reed standing before him. Reed's face was frozen in shock as he staggered backwards, managing a number of slow-motion steps until he collapsed. With blood pooling underneath him, Reed raised his head, eyes wide, trying to question Tom standing over him but unable to produce the words through the blood filling his throat.

As the tactical team continued to advance cautiously on the property a blur of a body moved swiftly across the window sightline.

"Hold! Hostile in view," one of the team confirmed, bringing the team to a silent standstill.

Just as quickly as the body was seen, the silence of the situation was punctured by two consecutive shots and a piercing scream sending the team to dive for cover on the floor instantly.

"Shots fired," the tactical leader confirmed. "Hold positions. I repeat, hold positions."

At the end of the driveway Ethan and Meadows both jumped instinctively at the sound of the shots. As Abbey's scream followed the double shot, Ethan looked at Meadows, unable to speak.

"Give me eyes up there," Meadows barked, "what the fuck is happening?"

"No, no, no," was all Ethan could manage.

"*It's not Swift,*" the radio confirmed, "*it wasn't engagement either. But no line on shooter or any victim.*"

Tom stood over Reed, watching as the final gargled breaths escaped from his fading form.

"Please try to be quiet," Tom said to Abbey. "That kind of noise really isn't helpful to anyone."

"Fuck you," Abbey managed through her own hyperventilation.

"And so the time has come." Tom smiled as he threw the gun to the floor next to his quarry and made his way behind the protection of Abbey, looking directly out of the window.

Abbey struggled to make her body swing again, trying to give those she knew were outside a split-second to take the fatal kill shot that could end everything in a moment. Tom grabbed her legs with one arm battling against the struggle and pushed his own legs tight against the side of Abbey's head, clamping her in place. Abbey feigned one final convulsion as she reached up to retrieve the wooden shard from her pocket, conceding defeat and letting her motion come to rest.

"You really think you're gonna get to walk away from this?"

"You really do think I'm senseless, don't you, Ms Swift?"

With his free hand Tom withdrew a hunting knife from his jacket and lowered himself down to Abbey's level, face to face.

"I do know you aren't walking away from this."

"And who is this to punish? Me for seeing you as just another member of the shower of shit you really are, or Ethan for ruining your work."

Tom brought the knife round, holding it tight against Abbey's neck, releasing a faint trickle of blood just from the pressure of the blade on her skin.

"It really is pathetic," Abbey added with a laugh. "Like you could go on forever and no one would know. As if you had this intelligence... What a dick."

Tom leant in close, whispering spittle into Abbey's ear through clenched teeth, "You have no idea, and I guess you never will..."

"You're getting emotional, Tom. Didn't you say you should never do that? Why so angry, Tom? Why? Or should I call you Tutor? We've read all your little messages, Tom. I'll be honest. I didn't have you down as a pervert. But Ethan called it, your need to have children and adolescents around you."

Tom sneered, loosening the pressure of the knife and calming his breathing as he returned his heartbeat closer to its resting state.

"Words and accusations aren't going to get you anywhere, Ms Swift."

As Abbey felt the pressure release against her throat, she violently convulsed again, taking Tom by surprise. Throwing her body to one side, she swung her arms back toward her hip where Tom remained, driving the shard in her hands down the side of his face and forcibly into the base of his neck and shoulder. Reeling backwards Tom screamed out in pain, trying to remove the shard with one hand while swinging the knife in the other and slicing Abbey's neck with a wild slash. Ignoring the shooting pain coursing down the side of her body, Abbey tried to lift herself up toward the ceiling beam, again knowing that time and gravity weren't going to be doing her any favours with her latest wound. Tom staggered to a halt, grabbing the wooden shard and pulling it from its implanted state, grimacing and shaking as he discarded it on the floor. Seething with rage and covered in blood, sweat and spittle, Tom lunged forward, arcing wildly in Abbey's direction but was distracted from his target as the glass of the window shattered with two bullets striking simultaneously in his lower neck and head, sending him into a crumpled heap on the floor. Abbey's struggles subsided, tears streaming into her hairline as she felt herself losing the fight with her own consciousness amid the noise and activity of a fully-armed tactical unit storming the property, laying hands on her neck and lowering her body against the cold floor.

CHAPTER FIFTY

Abbey was sat up in a hospital bed watching the news on a hired deep-set television, perched on a wall bracket in the corner of the room. With a dressing on her neck and a drip in her arm she kept moving from one to the other, rubbing at both. Ethan was sat on a bedside chair, admiring the collection of cards, flowers and chocolates from a mass of well-wishers.

"So which one's from you?" Abbey asked with a smile, looking at the collection of presents received.

"That one," Ethan replied, looking up at the television. "Can't imagine being in here without some form of distraction. Even if it is only five stations."

"What do you expect? The TV looks like it's from the 1980s!"

Ethan raised his eyebrows and sighed.

"Thank you though."

"So how long you in for? These things aren't cheap you know. Despite what you may think."

"Only a few days. This thing's mostly superficial," Abbey said, rubbing at her neck bandage again. "I think they just want to be sure."

"You had everyone worried."

"Everyone?" Abbey teased with a grin.

Ethan reddened slightly and turned his attention back to the screen in the corner.

"They'll be glad of the break from me," Abbey continued. "Besides, who doesn't love a bit of daytime TV and sick leave?"

Ethan mustered a half-hearted smile and squeezed Abbey's hand.

"What about you?" Abbey asked.

"What about me?" Ethan replied, turning his attention back to Abbey and keeping hold of her hand. "I'm fine."

"The job?" Abbey replied with a look suggesting that was obviously what she meant.

"Oh... They'd like me to come in as a permanent consultant."

"And?" Abbey said excitedly, squeezing Ethan's hand herself this time.

"I'm thinking about it," Ethan said with a broad smile.

THE END

ACKNOWLEDGEMENTS

This book wouldn't have come into being without the efforts and support from a number of different people. To all at Bloodhound Books, with special mentions to Betsy Reavley, Tara Lyons, Rachel Tyrer, Lexi Curtis and Hannah Deuce, thank you for making the whole process as painless as possible and showing as much passion in supporting the book as I could hope for. To Ian Skewis for his supportive words, keen eye and attention to detail in making the finished product the best that it could be.

To a couple of crucial individuals that wish to remain unnamed but helped to keep facts and processes within the realms of reality.

Everyone says it, but this wouldn't have been possible without the support of my wife, and first reviewer, Kathryn. Along with Beth, you are my two greatest achievements and staunchest supporters. Not too far behind them is my sister, who was convinced that this would happen. *Let it Rip!*

And finally, to you, for choosing this story amongst an ocean of choice. I hope I justified your decision, and you enjoyed the first of Ethan and Abbey's escapades. If you are keen to learn more about our fledgling heroes or wish to let me know your thoughts, please feel free to send me an email at scornwellbooks@yahoo.com. I will do my best to reply to all contacts.

ABOUT THE AUTHOR

Steve lives with his wife and daughter in Letchworth, Hertfordshire. Drawn to the darker side of fiction, he likes stories and adventures where thrills and suspense, without nonsensical filler, allow the characters to come alive and tell their tales.

An avid sports fan, whenever given the opportunity, he can be found on the golf course, spending time with family and attending country music gigs.

A NOTE FROM THE PUBLISHER

Thank you for reading this book. If you enjoyed it please do consider leaving a review on Amazon to help others find it too.

We hate typos. All of our books have been rigorously edited and proofread, but sometimes mistakes do slip through. If you have spotted a typo, please do let us know and we can get it amended within hours.

info@bloodhoundbooks.com

Printed in Great Britain
by Amazon

63195256R00160